Though the rocl[...]
once they were out o[...]
the nearest wall for su[...] [...]urned to stare at Robert
as he entered and quietly shut the door.

"Are you kidding? This is huge."

Robert cocked his head with a puzzled look. With a glance over her head, he surveyed the room and nodded.

"It is a rather large dining car, isn't it? We usually take our meal in our carriage."

Ellie shook her head. "No, I mean your group. This Victorian thing. The train. I assume you all hooked your cars up to the train at some point because I didn't see them when we left. How do you all do this? It must cost quite a bit."

With a slight shrug of his elegant shoulders, he searched her face with an expression not unlike a laboratory researcher studying his specimen. His lips twitched. "You say the strangest things, Miss Standish. I am not sure what you are asking."

She shot him a dark look and stomped her foot...just a bit. "Oh, stop this silly act, *Bobby*. Y'all are driving me nuts. I feel like I've landed in a madhouse."

Apparently unimpressed by her righteous rage, he chuckled and murmured in a low voice. "I am beginning to feel the same way, Miss Standish."

Reviews for Bess McBride

"A SIGH OF LOVE is a heartwarming story; a believable romance for two very lonely and deserving individuals. Touching, sweet, romantic and poignant, A SIGH OF LOVE has it all. This is a beautiful love story, one I will read again."
~*Scarlet*, Romance Junkies

"I just could not put it down. I highly recommend this book to anyone who wants to read a good love story with great action."
~*Brenda Talley*, The Romance Studio

In A SIGH OF LOVE, Bess McBride has once again delivered a heart-warming romance between two deserving people. The author's wonderful descriptions of Alaska provide the perfect backdrop for the story. I highly recommend A SIGH OF LOVE for anyone wanting a sweet, satisfying romance in a beautiful setting.
~*Ann Elizabeth Cree*

"I absolutely loved this story. Alaska was the perfect backdrop for this story and the characters were just so believable. I would definitely recommend this story to others and I eagerly look forward to reading more stories from Ms. McBride."
~*Diana*, Night Owl Romance

LOVE OF MY HEART is a wonderful, heart-warming story that had me rooting for the two couples all the way. The story threads are tied up in a most satisfying way. I eagerly look forward to reading more of Bess McBride.
~*Ann Elizabeth Cree*

The best part of this story is that true love endures. The author gives the reader a HEA that ties up all the loose ends, even the supernatural. Ms. McBride has an incredible turn of mind.
~*Michele*, The Long and Short of It

A
Train
Through
Time

by

Bess McBride

A Train Through Time

Cover Art by *Tamra Westberry*

The Wild Rose Press
PO Box 706
Adams Basin, NY 14410-0706
Visit us at www.thewildrosepress.com

Publishing History
First Vintage Rose Edition, 2008
Print ISBN 1-60154-301-8

Published in the United States of America

Dedication

To Cinnamon, Mike and Lily,
who waited for me at the library while I did the research,
and to Les
for listening to the story as it unfolded.

Prologue

"I'm not going to marry an eighteen-year-old girl, Grandmother." Robert turned away and strode to the bay window, where he stared down onto the city below.

"Robert, be reasonable. You need to marry sometime. Don't you want a wife? One young enough to give you children? Any one of your sister's friends would be quite suitable."

"I'm afraid not, Grandmother. I'm waiting."

"Waiting for what?" Mrs. Chamberlain demanded.

"The right one. She will come along. I know it."

"For goodness sake, Robert. Where will you find her? You never appear even to look."

Robert continued to stare out the window with his hands clasped behind his back. "I do not think I have met her yet, but I feel certain that I will know her when she does finally appear."

"Robert, what nonsense! You are usually so sensible in all matters, except when it comes to this subject. It seems my son's wife raised a silly romantic," the older woman muttered.

"Perhaps she did, Grandmother. Perhaps she did," he murmured with a soft smile.

"Give me great-grandchildren, Robert. I cannot live forever."

He turned away from the window and grinned at the frail-appearing, silver-haired woman resting on the green velvet settee.

"Yes, you will, Grandmother. You will outlive us all."

"Hmmppff." She looked away. "The house is quiet. We need children in it once again."

"Perhaps my sister can do the honors in a few years, Grandmother. All she lacks is a *suitable* husband." He consulted his pocket watch.

She eyed him with a piercing stare.

"Have you become a confirmed bachelor, Robert? Has

time passed you by, then?"

Robert laughed and bent to kiss his grandmother's pale cheek.

"I hope not, madam. I did not intend to remain a bachelor for the rest of my life."

"Then why do you wait? Give me a practical reason, none of your romantic musings."

He straightened and grinned. "I can only assure you once again that I wait for the *right* woman. I know it sounds foolish, but it is the truth." He turned toward the door. "I must go into the office to see to a few things before we leave tomorrow. I look forward to riding the train. I always do."

Chapter One

"Look at the mountain goats, Mom! Can you see them? Hurry, look!"

Ellie heard the boy's excited prattle from behind her seat and looked out the train window in time to catch sight of three white mountain goats perched precariously on a rock shelf on the craggy hills bordering the tracks. One brave goat nimbly jumped down to a lower ledge on the seemingly sheer cliff front. Ellie caught her breath and held it. The goat made a successful landing and immediately began nibbling on some tender morsel growing on the rock front.

"Did you see that, Mom? I can't believe it didn't fall. I wish we were coming here to Montana to visit, instead of going to Seattle."

A woman's voice murmured, "Shhh. Maybe we will, John. Maybe we will. Lay your head on the pillow and get some sleep. We'll be in Seattle in the morning, and then you can see Grandpa."

The view of the mountain goats receded into the dusky distance behind tall pine trees, and Ellie turned away from the window to stare down at the book in her lap, attempting once again to focus on the latest published papers on women's studies.

The voices behind her seat quieted, and she sighed. She agreed with the boy and wished she were coming to visit the magnificent Rocky Mountains instead of hurtling past to attend yet another boring seminar in Seattle.

"Women in the Pacific Northwest, Turn of the Century."

Ellie jumped slightly. Her elderly seatmate was a quiet gentleman who had spoken very little since she boarded the train in Chicago. His cultured voice startled her.

"That seems like rather heavy reading for a vacation." He favored her with a friendly smile.

3

Ellie glanced down at the book in her hand again, then up to his face with a sheepish grin.

"It isn't holding my interest, I'm afraid."

She studied him from under veiled lashes. Dark corduroy slacks flattered his charcoal turtleneck sweater. A silver watch adorned his left hand, which boasted a silver-colored wedding ring...the same silver that streaked his hair. Startlingly bright emerald green eyes met hers.

"Are you a student?"

She gave a quick shake of her head and nodded toward the book. "The teacher, I'm ashamed to say. I'm finding the book dull going. How can anyone take a vibrant era such as the turn of the century and make it so dull?" She shook her head and chuckled. "I'm doing some advance reading for a seminar I'm attending in Seattle."

She clamped her mouth shut, chatty soul that she was.

"Really? What kind of seminar?" He raised an elegant eyebrow.

She nodded toward the book again with a grin. "Women's Studies, Turn of the Century America."

"So you teach women's studies?"

"Yes, at Chicago Community College."

"I see. How interesting."

"Not really," she demurred. "And what brings you onto the train today?" She eyed him with interest.

"Oh, I'm heading home. I've just been on a visit to my daughter and grandchildren in Washington, D.C."

The passing vista of snow-capped peaks atop rocky mountains dotted with evergreen trees caught her eye once again. The sun had set, and the mountains turned a hazy purple in the waning light. She sighed at the beauty of the scenery before her.

"It's beautiful here, isn't it?"

He looked past her out the window. "It is. One of the reasons I prefer to take the train."

She flashed him a quick grin. "Me, too. I love trains. I'd take them all the time if I could. They just don't have enough routes anymore," she ended on a wistful note.

"They certainly had more when I was a boy, that's for sure. My folks traveled everywhere by train in the thirties. My grandparents, too. They took us to Glacier

National Park. But people have such busy lives today and no longer have time for the slower mode of travel." Green eyes twinkled as he gave her a whimsical smile.

Ellie nodded. "It's true. Every time I travel by train, I have to take extra time from work, but I do love it."

"So, why women's studies, may I ask?" He nodded toward the book in her lap.

Warmth tinged her cheeks. "Oh, I don't know. I've always found the subject interesting. Well, I would, of course. I'm a woman." She smiled crookedly. "I guess I'm what you would call a feminist. I don't really like the term, but you get the idea. I like the subject of women, their importance in history, their value in the world, and I want to pass that enthusiasm on to others, so I teach." She gave him a small self-deprecating smile. "I'm especially fascinated by women's lives at the turn of the century, but I'm finding this book a bit dry." She wiggled the book and wrinkled her nose.

"May I see it?" he asked.

She blinked and handed it to him.

He opened the cover and perused the index, stopping occasionally to smile.

"Corsets: Curves or Curses." He chuckled as he read the chapter heading aloud. "Well, that certainly doesn't sound dry." He handed the book back to her.

She grinned. "You should read the chapter titled "Hair: Halo or Hell on Earth." I can't believe women tortured their hair as much as they did in the name of fashion." Ellie virtually spat out the last word, then reined in her unruly tongue, though not before she saw the twinkle in her companion's eyes.

"Perhaps not all women in those days had your lovely brown hair." His appreciative glance brought a blush to her cheeks, and she tossed her head as if to shake off embarrassment.

"Thank you," she murmured, completely thrown off her feminist seat for a moment. She gave him a sideways glance. He appeared to be in his mid-eighties, but his full head of silver hair and bright green eyes left no doubt he'd once been a very handsome man...and still was, for that matter.

His eyes...

The twinkle continued, and for a moment, she had the craziest notion she'd seen those eyes before.

"Have we met? Have you been to Chicago? This may sound strange, but you seem familiar to me in some way."

"No, I don't think so. I've never gotten off the train in Chicago." He drew his brows together in a puzzled expression. "You know, I have to say you look familiar, as well. I wonder where we could have met."

Ellie shook her head slowly, searching his face for a clue. "I don't know. It's odd, isn't it?" She reached out a hand. "I'm sorry. I should have introduced myself. Ellie Standish." She grinned.

"Edward Richardson. It's nice to meet you." He gripped her hand in a surprisingly firm, warm clasp.

"And you," she murmured, reluctantly pulling her hand from his grasp, aware of an inexplicable desire to let it linger there a while.

Though handsome for a man his age, he had to be nearly fifty years her senior, and she found her blossoming attraction to him somewhat uncomfortable. Kyle would laugh, she thought, arrogantly unable to see that his fiancée might find other men attractive, even older men in their eighties. She dropped her eyes to the book in her lap, feeling slightly foolish and hoping she hadn't developed some sort of father fixation on her seat companion.

"Are you from Chicago?" Edward cocked his head to the side in a charming inquiry, eyes attentive with apparent interest.

"No, I've lived in many different places. I moved to Chicago to take the job at the college after I graduated from university."

"How do you like Chicago?"

"It's a big city," she sighed. "Fast paced...probably too fast for me. It seems all I have time to do is go to work and come home, go to work and come home." She raised her eyes to his sympathetic face.

"I know what you mean. Washington, D.C. is hectic, as well. Although Seattle is a big town, I do find it a bit more relaxing. It has grown tremendously since I was a boy."

"Have you always lived in Seattle?"

6

"All my life, since 1921."

"I can't imagine living in one place that long," Ellie sighed wistfully, "but I often wonder what it would be like." She turned to look out the window as statuesque dark evergreens guarded the darkening hills above the moving train.

"Do you move a lot, Ellie?"

The intimate sound of her name on his gentle voice startled her. The question embarrassed her. It always did. She had no Romanian blood, as far she knew, but her gypsy soul would not sit quietly still...much to her regret.

"I do. I can't seem to stay in one place for long. I've been in Chicago for three years now, and I've got itchy feet. These little breaks to travel to seminars help ease the pain of trying to stay put." She gave the older man a quirky grin. "My fiancé, Kyle, is the only thing keeping me from dashing off in search of a new life, a new adventure."

"Your fiancé?" Edward's expressive eyebrows rose. "Congratulations. When are you planning to marry?"

Ellie's eyes flickered away from his before she replied airily. "Oh, we haven't set a date yet. I'm busy and so is he. He's an investment banker."

"How did you meet?"

She colored. "At a bar, of all places. I was out drinking with a few friends. He was there with friends." She shrugged carelessly. "What about you, Edward? Are you married?" Her eyes traveled to the gleaming silver band on his left hand.

His eyes followed hers. With the fingers of his right hand, he gently caressed the band, the gesture suggesting love.

"I was. I feel like I still am." Green eyes met hers. "She passed away last year."

"Oh, Edward. I'm sorry."

"Thank you. It's been difficult." With a brief smile in her direction, Edward turned away to gaze out the window on the other side of the train.

Ellie surreptitiously studied his profile, open and friendly only a moment ago, now closed and somber. She didn't take his withdrawal personally. The working of his jaw revealed emotions he struggled to control. She still couldn't shake the familiar feeling she'd seen him before. Forcing herself to turn away, she picked up her book again with a renewed earnest determination to make some headway in her reading. She stared at the words on the pages, each one blending into the next, unable to concentrate on the task at hand.

A glance from under her eyelashes to the left revealed Edward's eyes were closed. He appeared intent on sleep. She sighed and turned toward the window. Her pale face, softly highlighted by the overhead lights, reflected in the glass. The passing scenery faded into darkness with only an occasional twinkling light visible in the distance. She leaned her head against the cool glass and closed her eyes.

Drowsily, she wondered if Kyle were sleeping. For the last year, he'd adopted the habit of going to bed promptly at 10 p.m. and leaving the apartment by 7 a.m. to catch the El. Since she barely got home from class by 9 at night, she hardly saw him. Her absence to attend the seminar in Seattle would hardly be noticed in his busy world. It didn't matter. The first flush of love had long gone, leaving the makings of a long and boring marriage in its wake. But she was determined to follow through with the wedding, if and when she ever set a date. She was tired of moving, tired of being alone, tired of staring at an unknown future and ready to settle down—or ready to settle, at least.

Chapter Two

An unfamiliar jolt of the train awakened Ellie. Her eyes flew open. For the most part, the train ride had been smooth, the huge silver giant effortlessly gliding along the tracks with few sounds other than an occasional whistle and no untoward movements.

Blearily, she looked out the window. Darkness had given way to dawn, and a soft rosy glow peeped through the tall evergreens which continued to grace the landscape. Softly misted mountains appeared in the distance. She glanced at her watch. Four more hours to Seattle.

With a crick in her neck, Ellie straightened and raised her arms above her head. She turned to ask Edward how he'd slept, but his seat was empty. In fact, something seemed to be wrong with his seat. She rubbed the sleep from her eyes and stared at it again. Something was definitely wrong. Where was the armrest she'd leaned on the night before? She ran a hand along the seat cushion, and her eyes widened at the rich look and feel of the red velvet along the bench.

Bench? Had she wandered into another car in the night? Where was she?

A buzz of female voices from the rear penetrated her consciousness, and she craned her neck to see over the back of her seat, or rather, her bench. Six or seven young women lounged about on plush antique rattan furniture in various poses—some perched on the edge of their seats, prim and proper with clasped hands, others balanced teacups above saucers, while another young lady leaned over a pink velvet sofa and whispered to a blonde woman. An occasional tinkling laugh behind a discreet hand broke the steady hum of chatter.

Ellie blinked and stared at their clothing. Huge hats, festooned with feathers and flowers, towered above small heads supported by long delicate necks. As a group, the young women wore a similar style of clothing, with high-collared white lacy blouses. Some wore tailored dark jackets. Ellie's startled eyes traveled the length of their skirts—long, flowing garments in varying shades of dark colors that covered all but the tips of their shoes. The woman who stood had an impossibly tiny waist.

With a pounding heart and a dry mouth, Ellie slid down out of sight. What was going on? She backed into the corner of the bench with her face pressed against the velvet of the upholstered bench back. She strained to make out words but could hear only the lilting rhythm of the women's voices, broken by the timbre of an occasional male voice. She hadn't seen any men on first glance. Ellie rubbed her sweating palms on her denim skirt and dragged in an uneven breath. The rumbling of the train along the tracks proved she was still onboard, albeit the carriage rocked and swayed more than it had the night before. An unusual odor permeated the air—the pleasant smell of cooked food combined with...was it...coal?

Ellie chewed a corner of her lower lip nervously and pressed even more tightly into the corner of her seat, hoping to make herself invisible. She studied the carriage door just in front of her bench as it rattled with the motion of the train. Constructed of a large pane of antique leaded glass framed by dark varnished wood, the elegant door allowed as much light to stream in as possible, given the narrow confined space between cars. Lovely as it was, she hoped fervently the door wouldn't open to expose her presence to a newcomer entering the room. Fairly sure she'd unwittingly trespassed onto a first-class lounge, she wondered how on earth she'd managed to sleepwalk her way into a luxurious car that smacked of turn-of-the-century style.

The sound of a man's cheerful laughter caught her ear. Against her better judgment and free will, she slid up on one knee and peeked over the back of the seat to survey the scene behind her again. Her widened eyes homed in on the author of the husky laugh as he leaned against the leaded glass door at the back of the carriage. She gasped against the velvet upholstery of the seat back, mild hysteria robbing her of breath.

A dark head of well-groomed, thick, wavy chestnut

hair crowned a handsome angular face. He smiled broadly at a woman seated in a chair nearby. The generous smile should have held her attention, but she couldn't take her eyes off his attire. A dark blue jacket hung carelessly open to reveal a gray vest over a white high collar shirt. Matching dark blue trousers revealed long, lean legs that began at a slender waist and seemed to travel forever until they ended at the tips of highly polished black boots.

Mr. Debonair pulled a watch on a chain from a pocket in his vest and consulted it. With a devastating smile, he leaned down to the young beauty at his side and spoke in a low voice. Ellie's ears perked at the woman's tinkling laugh. It seemed restrained, lacking gusto and spontaneity. She could not see her face clearly in the back of the car.

Ellie lowered herself back into her seat, willing herself to miniaturize, and turned a speculative eye on the stylish door in front, leading to the next car. The door looked as though it opened outward instead of sliding open as did the rest of the train's compartments. A brass handlebar preserved the glass from unruly fingerprints.

Ellie gathered her courage as she imagined a scene where she bolted through the door and escaped into the next carriage. If she acted quickly enough, the oddly-dressed passengers would never see or hear anything except the sound of the door closing behind her. If the next car turned out to be first class, she would feign ignorance—which was true—and ask to be directed back to her seat in coach.

She lowered her feet to the carpeted floor and slid to the edge of her seat, no easy task on velvet. Just as she prepared to spring for the door, it opened wide. She fell back against her seat. A strong smell of coal assaulted her nose before the door shut quietly behind the newcomer. A white-coated waiter of African descent precariously balanced china on a round silver serving tray with the palm of one hand while securing the door behind his back with the other.

Ellie scooted back into her corner, but the motion caught the waiter's eye as he took a step forward. He stared down at her, dark eyes widening at the sight of the stowaway.

"Ah, tea is here. Come, come, young man, bring it here. We've been waiting for quite some time for refreshment, and I must say I'm quite parched." A querulous female voice rung out.

Ellie hunched her head into her shoulders like a turtle and gave the startled young man an uneasy grin. With a plea in her eyes, she raised a finger to her lips and shook her head.

He hesitated and blinked at her, obviously debating what to do. Ellie mouthed the word "please" as she continued to shake her head.

"Young man." The impatient elderly female voice forced a decision on him. He furrowed his brow, gave a slight shake of his head and moved past the bench toward the open seating area of the car.

Ellie held her breath, wondering if anyone was going to come around the corner and demand her instant removal. She would be too happy to comply, she thought, as she eyed the door once again. She considered the wiser plan would be to exit in the waiter's wake. It seemed likely no one would follow the young man's progress out of the carriage.

"Ahh, there you are." The older woman seemed temporarily appeased by the arrival of her tea. Ellie didn't remember seeing any senior citizens on her quick survey of the passengers. "Yes, that's it. Two sugars will do. Thank you."

Ellie strained to hear the handsome man's voice for the first time, but the tinkle of teacups on saucers and the hum of muted voices drowned him out. She kept an eye on the aisle, preparing for a quick exit with the waiter.

Within moments, he returned to peer around the edge of her seat. She peeked up at him. His white cotton, brass-buttoned tunic jacket gleamed over a clean, ankle-length white apron which covered dark trousers. He gripped the now-empty tray tightly in both hands.

"Miss, what are you doing in here?" he hissed. "I don't think you're supposed to be here, are you?" The young waiter threw a quick glance over his shoulder.

Ellie hunched her shoulders and shook her head. She matched the hush of his whisper.

"I don't know what I'm doing here. I went to sleep in

my seat last night and woke up here this morning. Seat 31B. Do you know where that is? Can I follow you back?"

Dark brown eyes blinked. "31B? I don't know where that seat is, miss. I've never heard of it. I think I'd better find the conductor and bring him to you."

"Oh, yes, that's a good idea. Please do. Actually, let me come with you. He'll figure out where my seat is. So, is this like some kind of reenactment thing?" She moved to the edge of her seat to rise, her hand roaming the seat behind her in search of her purse. Oh, surely, she had her purse!

"Reenactment?" He raised his eyebrows and shook his head inquiringly.

"Yeah, you know, like Civil War reenactments. Where they all dress up in period costumes, act out historical scenarios?" She dropped her eyes to search the corners of her seat. Where was her purse?

"Steward, is anything wrong?"

The close proximity of the masculine voice startled Ellie, and she jerked and twisted around to find Mr. Debonair staring straight down at her as he stood behind the bench.

The steward backed up toward the door with a subservient nod in the well-dressed man's direction. He clutched the tray to his chest.

"No, nothing's wrong, Mr. Chamberlain. This lady seems to be lost. I think she's from one of the other cars, you know, the immigrant cars. I don't know how she got in here. I'm gonna go get the conductor. He'll take her back where she belongs."

Ellie flung an astonished look in the steward's direction. *Immigrant?* What was he talking about?

"I see. Well, miss, how did you find your way to this car?"

Mr. Chamberlain came around to the front of the bench. His green eyes ran up and down the length of her body with a frank appraising gaze, and Ellie took offense. She jumped up from her seat.

"Now just a minute there, Mr...uh...Chamberlain." She drew herself up to her entire five foot two inches and lifted her chin. "First off, you can drop that eyeing me up and down thing. It's very rude and typically male." An arch of one of his dark eyebrows did not deter her. "And another thing. Though this may be first class, it's not your train or your passenger car, and frankly, it's none of your business. So, if you don't mind, I'll just be off with the steward here."

The young steward gaped at her. He pressed himself into the thick glass door as if wishing he could disappear.

"Oh no, miss. You can't come with me," he whispered. "It's not safe."

Ellie twisted around to look behind her and caught a quick impression of the room in its entirety. Teacups stilled as the group of hat-festooned female heads looked up. She gritted her teeth, tightened her lips in a semblance of a smile, nodded in their direction and turned to face the steward.

"Oh, sure it is. I've traveled by train many times. So, let's go."

"Just a moment, miss." She stilled at the sound of Mr. Chamberlain's velvety voice. She glanced over her shoulder, unwilling to give him the satisfaction of turning around to face him. Why should she?

"Yes, Mr. Chamberlain?"

He dipped his head to the side in a motion that cut into her anger with its charming boyishness. "I apologize, madam. You are quite right. No matter where your seat on this train, I did not have the right to stare at you so boldly. I would not have done so with any other woman in this carriage."

"Thank you," Ellie murmured with a regal nod in his direction which belied her inner turmoil. The man certainly was smooth. "And now, if you don't mind, I'm leaving." Ellie turned toward the door. Seeing the steward still frozen in place with wide eyes, she pushed against the bar and opened the door to an unexpected blast of wind. Determined to leave with some semblance of huffy dignity, she hurriedly stepped out of the car, then reared back and faltered when she realized that the connector was covered only by some sort of canvas tarp, allowing a roaring wind to rush through the unsealed seams of the canvas. She stared at the uneven jostling between the two cars and wondered how she was going to manage to jump the crosswalk without losing her balance. With nothing to hold onto, Ellie braced herself against the wall, dizzy from the sight of the uneven dance of the connectors between the two cars, nauseated from the smell of coal and the increased rocking of the car on the platform. Her knees buckled.

A strong hand grasped her around the waist in a reassuring grip. Though she wore a bulky turtleneck sweater, the warmth of his hand seemed to sear her skin.

"Steady now, madam." Mr. Chamberlain decisively hauled her back into the carriage. His accomplice, the steward, shut the door behind them and posted himself as a sentry.

Ellie stared up at her handsome would-be rescuer as he lowered her back to the seat. He bent down to peer into her face.

"Are you well, madam? Though you stalked very prettily out of here, you seemed a bit shaky on the platform. I thought it best to bring you back inside." Twinkling green eyes belied the note of concern in his voice.

Ellie nodded, tongue-tied by his nearness. Her eyes locked on the cleft in his chin—a feature which gave his lean face a virile masculinity at odds with the fancy costume party she'd inadvertently crashed. His easy grin compelled an answering smile, and she clamped her lips together and fought against his obvious magnetism.

"Bobby, what is going on here? Who is this?"

Bobby's conversation partner, a young woman with golden hair swept up into a glorious Gibson-style hairdo, peered around the corner. She stared wide-eyed at a shrinking Ellie, who subconsciously raised a hand to tidy her own mop of curly brown hair, hopefully still tied back in a braid down her back.

Bobby straightened. "Nothing to worry about, Melinda. This unfortunate woman strayed onto our car by accident, probably at the last stop. The steward was just about to locate the conductor for us." He turned to the young waiter still guarding the door. "What is your name, young man?"

"Samuel, sir." Samuel dipped his head. "But, no, sir, I didn't bring her here. No, sir. I found her sitting right there." He bobbed his head up and down.

Ellie cringed. Good gravy! What was the matter with the young fellow? He seemed so nervous. Did he think he'd lose his job? Surely, they had a union! She sprang to his defense.

"That's right. Samuel didn't—"

"Samuel, would you be so good as to find the conductor and bring him here?" Mr. Chamberlain glanced down at Ellie with a dancing light in his eyes. "Our guest still seems a bit shaken from the jostling between the cars, and I think she should take a cup of tea with us here."

"Bobby?" Melinda moved forward to stare at Ellie with frank curiosity. "Are you sure that's wise?" Her sweet smile took the sting from her words. "I mean...what if someone is looking for her...perhaps her...em...people from the other cars?"

Ellie rolled her eyes and struggled to rise, though it seemed that three people hovered in her confined space all of a sudden, making it almost impossible for her to get up unless someone moved. She sank back down.

"Listen, y'all." She felt compelled to drawl, though she'd never lived in the South in her life. "I'm just fine, and I can find the conductor on my own. I can't imagine how I wandered onto this car in the first place. I don't have any *people*." She tossed a quick glance at darling Melinda. "And I don't need your tea. I don't even like tea. So if you will just excuse me, I'll get out of your hair."

Melinda broke out into the laugh that Ellie recognized from moments before. Her laugh certainly seemed spontaneous, but she repressed it behind a graceful hand.

"Nonsense, madam. You'll do no such thing. You cannot travel between the cars. I insist that you sit down at once, until I'm certain you feel better."

Ellie glared up at Bobby. His six-foot frame might intimidate other women, but she had no doubt she could jump up and wriggle past him to escape through the door. If only she could cross to the other car. What kind of carnival train was she on, anyway?

"I'm perfectly fine, *Bobby*." The name hardly suited him. "Just a drop in my blood sugar, I'm sure. I probably just need to eat something."

Bobby inclined his head in a gesture that smacked faintly of arrogance. "My name is *Robert* Chamberlain, madam. *Robert.* Only my irrepressibly spoiled sister calls me Bobby...and always against my wishes."

"What is going on up there, Robert?" The quavering voice of the elderly woman seemed strong enough to reach the front of the car, though thankfully she did not appear, as well.

A faint hint of lavender wafted into Ellie's nose, and she twisted her neck upward to see several more young women peering over the top and around the corner of her bench. The large beribboned and feathered hats bumped into one another as they ogled her with curiosity.

Ellie hunched into her seat, her cheeks burning. She suddenly understood how animals felt in a zoo. Hopefully, these women wouldn't start petting her.

"It seems we have an unexpected guest, Grandmother." Robert favored Ellie with a considering gaze while he allowed his voice to carry to the rear of the train. "A woman lost her way on the train and found herself in our carriage by accident. She feels a bit unwell at the moment."

Ellie glared at him, her chaotic thoughts struggling to form choice responses.

"Well, bring her back here, Robert. Let me look at her. I'd be grateful for a new diversion."

Ellie's eyes widened and she opened her mouth to retort, but Robert managed to beat her to it.

"I doubt she considers herself a diversion, Grandmother, but with your permission, I will bring her back for a cup of tea to help settle her nerves."

Robert gave Melinda a look, and she immediately jumped into action. "Okay, ladies, why don't we return to the lounge so Miss...er...the nice lady can come and have a cup of tea?" She skillfully shepherded the women away, to the increased sound of high-pitched questions.

"I don't know, ladies..." Melinda's voice trailed off as she moved away.

Ellie glanced back up at the two men staring at her. Robert nodded at Samuel, who gave Ellie a last sympathetic glance before pushing open the door to cross over to the next car. She would have followed, but Robert

17

managed to block her way without really seeming to do so. He casually leaned against the doorjamb in a relaxed fashion but with a presence reminiscent of a stone wall.

She slumped, sudden exhaustion overcoming her desire for flight.

Chapter Three

"May I help you up?" Robert moved away from the door and extended a hand to help her rise. Ellie stared at the well-groomed hand for a moment before she reluctantly took hold.

"I'm just waiting for the conductor. That's all. *Then* I'll be on my way."

"Certainly, Miss...em..." He extended his arm for her to take, but she pretended not to see as she glanced down and brushed imaginary wrinkles from her skirt. Out of the corner of her eye, she caught his wry expression and half smile as he dropped the supportive arm to his side.

"Ellie," she murmured. "Ellie Standish."

"Miss Standish." With an elegant wave of his hand, he indicated she should precede him toward the back of the car.

"Mr. Chamberlain." She moved past him with a straight back. Her moment of dignity vanished when she tripped on the unexpectedly plush red and gold oriental carpeting underfoot.

Robert's hand shot out to take her arm and steady her. With a burning face, she righted herself, nodded thanks and pulled her arm from his warm grasp.

Ellie moved into the center of the room where the occupants of the lounge alternately stood or sat. An elderly woman in a dark, high-necked, Victorian-style silk dress presided on a red velvet-cushioned rattan loveseat. She signaled Ellie forward.

"Come, girl. Sit here." With an incline of the large, dark beribboned hat on her head, she indicated Ellie should sit in the single chair beside her own.

Ellie paused, unwilling to be spoken to in such a bossy way, and equally unwilling to offend a senior citizen...especially a woman who apparently thought she had some sort of regal power. Acutely aware she was the center of attention as she hovered in the middle of the room, Ellie swallowed her pride, moved quickly to the luxurious chair and sat down.

Robert returned to his original position at the back door to lean against it with crossed arms. Ellie watched several pairs of admiring female eyes follow his progress and she understood their message. He presented a dashing figure—straight out of some Victorian romance in his well-tailored and immaculate dark blue coat and trousers.

"So, what is this I hear about you stowing away on our carriage, miss?"

Ellie's bemused eyes flew to the older woman's arrogant face. She appeared to be in her late seventies, though her costume made it difficult to guess an accurate age. Sharp blue eyes appraised Ellie steadily.

"Listen, Mrs. Chamberlain, is it?" The older woman tipped her head in a slight nod. "Well, listen, Mrs. Chamberlain. I'm not a *stowaway* per se. I'm not sure how I came to be in *your carriage*, but as I've told your grandson over there, I'm more than happy to be on my way."

Ellie looked across the room to see Melinda's eyes widen with apprehension. Let the girl worry. She had no intention of being bullied any more by these strange characters.

She returned her challenging gaze to Mrs. Chamberlain's face. Two red spots appeared on the older woman's cheeks.

The smell of coal must have blurred Ellie's common sense because she didn't quit there.

"I didn't really know people had *carriages* of their own these days. But if you have leased this one, then I'm sorry to have stumbled onto it. As I said, I'm ready to skedaddle, but *Bobby* here kept me from leaving with Samuel."

"Samuel?" Mrs. Chamberlain wrinkled her forehead with an eye toward Robert.

"The steward," Robert murmured from his position along the wall.

"The steward? What does he have to do with all of this?"

"Nothing. He just happened to see me in the seat up

there." Ellie jerked her head in the direction of the front of the car. "He seems very worried, by the way. You aren't going to try to get him in trouble, are you? Because he didn't do anything."

"Good gracious! What is she talking about? Robert? Melinda, pour the woman some tea, will you, dear?"

Melinda sprang into action and picked up an empty teacup and saucer from the table in front of the loveseat on the opposite wall.

A rustle of skirts and quiet murmurs left a befuddled Ellie with a quick impression that all of the other women resumed their seats. Only a lone dark-haired woman in a white shirtwaist blouse and dark brown skirt remained standing near Robert.

"Samuel will be fine, Miss Standish." Robert surveyed her with continuing amusement. Even from this distance, emerald sparks lit up his eyes.

"Standish, you say?" Mrs. Chamberlain turned crinkled eyes back to Ellie, who tore her gaze away from Robert once again. "That's a fine old name in American history. Are you related? How is it that you come to be traveling in the immigrant section, then?"

Ellie reached up to rub her temples. A headache seemed imminent.

"I don't think I'm related to Miles Standish, if that's what you mean. If I am, it's probably through some illegitimate offspring or something. And I don't know what you mean by *immigrant* section. Are you talking about a coach section? Trains don't have class systems anymore. Thank goodness."

Ellie rattled on, only slightly aware of several gasps from the other side of the room. She turned toward the unusually silent young women and noticed that several ladies stared down at the carpeting with rosy cheeks.

"Young woman, we do not speak that way in public. I can see that you probably are indeed from the working class. Please refrain from any further unsavory comments while in my carriage."

Melinda rose and crossed the room with Ellie's tea, the delicate cup rattling in the saucer. Ellie looked up to see the young blonde biting her lower lip and shaking her head ever so slightly as she met Ellie's eyes. Ellie reached for the cup, forgetting she didn't want the tea. With a cautious look in her grandmother's direction, Melinda swished her way back to her seat.

Ellie stared down into her cup and took a deep breath.

"I'm sorry, Mrs. Chamberlain. I didn't mean to offend you. I just don't know what you mean by an *immigrant* section."

"That is not the offense to which I referred, Miss Standish."

Robert interceded, a hint of laughter in his voice. "I believe my grandmother referred to the...ah...suggestion that Miles Standish might have had an...em...indiscretion. Isn't that so, Grandmother?"

"Robert, that sort of talk does not bode well for you, either."

Ellie stared at two deep dimples in Robert's angular cheeks. Although seemingly a domineering, arrogant man—much like his grandmother—the whimsical dimples warmed his face and made her heart flutter. The teacup rattled in the saucer as her hand trembled. She lowered the cup to the teak occasional table beside her seat.

"Um, do y'all have any bottled water, by chance?"

Heads turned toward one another. "Bottled water?" Melinda murmured.

"Yeah, you know, just some water. I've got the worst headache."

Melinda half rose, her sympathetic face filled with concern.

"Sit down, Melinda, there's a good girl. Miss Standish, I don't think we have anything such as *bottled* water. Would you care for a lemonade instead? When the steward comes back, he can fetch one for you."

Ellie rubbed her temples once again. "No, no, thank you, Mrs. Chamberlain. By then, the conductor will have come to get me, and I can get back to my seat and my purse and get something for my headache."

"I see." The older woman nodded. "Drink some tea. The hot water will help clear your headache."

Ellie gave her a quick smile and nodded. Would the conductor ever come? She picked up the delicate pink-and-gold-decorated porcelain teacup again and swallowed the hot liquid. It did feel pleasant in her dry mouth.

"Miss Standish. If you're not in the immigrant section...and forgive us for assuming so, are you in tourist class?" Melinda spoke from across the room. "I've seen that carriage before...once."

"I think there is some confusion as to what carriage Miss Standish was on, and I do not think she feels up to resolving the matter at the moment. Perhaps we should let her sip her tea in comfort for a few minutes before we assail her with more questions."

Ellie turned toward the voice of the dark-haired female who stood next to Robert. A beautiful woman who appeared to be in her late thirties, she stood almost as tall as Robert. Her slender build showed off her costume to great advantage. She regarded Ellie with dark-lashed, warm brown eyes and a pleasant curve of her full lips.

"A friend of the family, Mrs. Constance Green." Robert made the introduction with familiarity. Ellie's heart skipped a beat. When he looked at Constance, his grin took on an affectionate twist.

Constance nodded in greeting but did not move forward. Ellie studied the heightened color on the beauty's face, her feminine instincts telling her that Constance was interested in Robert. She bit back a small sigh of disappointment. She wasn't surprised. The man certainly was handsome!

Ellie nodded gratefully to Constance and took another sip of the surprisingly brisk tea.

"I really don't know what's taking the conductor so long to get here. I'm sure he'll get me back to my car and my seat, and I can get out of your hair. You must have things you want to do."

"I doubt if the conductor will arrive before our next stop, at Wenatchee. Unless he was in the dining carriage next door, Samuel will not be able to contact him until he can make his way to the carriages further down."

"Yes, I'm sure that's quite true, Grandson. You'll just have to settle in for a bit, Miss Standish. We won't reach Wenatchee for another hour yet."

"An hour?" Ellie looked from Robert to his grandmother. "Really? Well, why can't Samuel just call the conductor? I really should make my way next door to find out what's going on." She attempted to rise but Mrs. Chamberlain laid a restraining hand on her arm for just a brief second before removing it.

"No, Miss Standish. That's not possible. It's not safe."

Mrs. Chamberlain's words reawakened a vivid picture of the funhouse connection between the trains. Never one for such carnival rides, Ellie didn't know if she would make the crossing in one piece. She slumped back into her chair and picked up her tea to toss off the last dregs. Uncomfortably aware that the women on the other side of the room continued to stare at her, she set her cup down, lowered her eyes and busily picked at a loose thread on her skirt.

"Miss Standish, forgive me, but I was wondering. What material is your skirt? I haven't seen one like that before."

A younger woman about Melinda's age gazed at Ellie with an earnest expression. Her blue hat with decorative netting contrasted wonderfully with golden chestnut hair.

Ellie suspected she'd fallen into a wormhole. What kind of a question was that?

"Denim. You know? A jeans skirt?" She hunched her shoulders self-consciously. "I know they're a bit old-fashioned, but I like them. They're comfortable for traveling."

Melinda giggled. "See, Amy, I told you it was called denim...like serge. A sturdy fabric used by dockworkers and such." She turned to Ellie. "Did you make the skirt yourself, Miss Standish? I've never seen this material in a skirt before."

Ellie stared at the characters before her with narrowed eyes. Was this some elaborate hoax?

"No, I bought it, Melinda. Just like you can buy denim skirts in your local department store." The gig was up! Ellie crossed her arms and leaned back in her seat. She avoided looking at Robert, knowing he would continue the charade.

"I must say, you all are certainly deep in character. Is this some sort of Victorian reenactment I've wandered into?" She scanned the eyes of the women across the room, daring them to continue the lie.

"Reenactment?" Amy's young forehead wrinkled. "I

beg your pardon?"

"Oh, please, ladies and...gentleman. You know, like a Civil War reenactment or a Mountain Man rendezvous." She continued to avoid Robert's eyes, though she was acutely aware he watched her. "I'm just exhausted and confused enough to believe in all this. You've had your fun, though. Are you a period piece ensemble on tour? Oh, wait, I know! One of those mystery dinner theater groups!" Ellie clapped her hands, thankful to have found an explanation for her bizarre companions. She ignored the lack of affirmative response. "Well, y'all have done a wonderful job. I almost...I gotta tell you...I almost thought for a moment...I'd stepped back in time. Good job!"

"Miss Standish, what are you babbling about?" Mrs. Chamberlain turned toward her grandson. "Robert, I don't think she's well. Come see if she has a fever. No, on second thought, don't. She might carry some sort of contagious disease."

Ellie shook her head warningly at Robert, but he dutifully crossed the carriage and put a hand to her forehead. His touch tingled. She jumped back into her seat and swatted at his hand.

"That's enough, thank you, Robert. I'm just fine. All right, you guys, so how 'bout that bottled water? Can I have some now?"

"She has no fever, Grandmother, though it appears her hazel eyes are flashing fire." With a playful grin, he chuckled and ran a finger lightly across her cheek before he moved away.

Ellie jumped up in agitation. "All right, y'all. I'll admit that I'm going to have a hard time getting to the next car. I'm petrified to cross that itty bitty thing between us, but I'm ready to head out." She ignored the well-acted stunned expressions on their faces and turned to head toward the door. A sudden thought struck her, and she rotated to face the group. "You know, I teach women's studies. The turn of the century is one of my areas of interest. What a coincidence that I should meet you all, eh? Too funny!" She dipped a quick curtsey in deference to the theme. "Thanks for the tea, and thanks for the show. It's been great."

Ellie spun away and made a beeline for the door

before anyone tried to stop her. She pushed the heavy door open and stepped out onto the narrow connector between the two cars. Snapping the door shut behind her, she hesitated on the landing as she stared wide eyed at the precarious, wildly moving floor between the two cars. Wind rushed through the connector—wind and the dense smell of coal. She moved forward with a tentative step, preparing herself for a balancing act extraordinaire as she crossed the rocking corridor. That there was no way she could fall to her death on the tracks below did nothing to ease her fear of heights and fast moving, rocking trains.

She heard the door open behind her but refused to turn around. If anything, the sound gave her the impetus to jump across the uneven connection in a single motion. She steadied herself on the opposite landing.

"Well, Miss Standish, I see you made it across safely. I was worried about you." Robert raised his voice to make himself heard above the rumbling on the tracks and the whistling of the wind.

She turned to face him. With legs apart, he stood with effortless balance...of course.

"Oh, I'm fine, thank you very much." It seemed obvious her words faded on the wind, because he frowned and gave his head a slight shake.

She cupped one hand to her mouth to shout. "Yes, I'm fine, thank you. See ya!" Ellie turned away and stopped short with surprise. Facing yet another old-fashioned wooden door, she reached for the brass handle. The hairs on the back of her neck tingled. She knew he watched her. An unexpected sway of the carriage threw her off balance again, and she staggered against the closed door on the side of the landing.

As she attempted to right herself on the lurching train, she saw Robert nimbly step across the connector. He grasped her hand and reached around her waist with the other to brace her body against his as an increased bout of rocking overtook the train.

He spoke near her ear. "Here, now. I have you. You really should have asked for help, Miss Standish. I don't think you have your train legs yet."

Unnerved by the unexpected thrill that shot through her at his touch, she attempted to pull away. With a sigh,

Robert kept firm hold on her and reached for the door.

"All right, madam. If you insist. By all means, let's see if we can find the conductor in the dining carriage." He pulled open the door and released her. Ellie stumbled through the entrance and entered another nightmare. White linen tablecloths with vases of flowers brightened dining tables hosting yet more people in Victorian dress. Several African-American stewards moved through the length of the car, ably balancing plates of food on large round trays. The ornate décor of the dining car matched the lounge car with the glow of highly varnished wood walls and ceiling, brass fittings and red/orange oriental carpeting.

Though the rocking motion of the car eased once they were out of the connector, Ellie leaned against the nearest wall for support. She turned to stare at Robert as he entered and quietly shut the door.

"Are you kidding? This is huge."

Robert cocked his head with a puzzled look. With a glance over her head, he surveyed the room and nodded.

"It is a rather large dining car, isn't it? We usually take our meal in our carriage."

Ellie shook her head. "No, I mean your group. This Victorian thing. The train. I assume you all hooked your cars up to the train at some point, because I didn't see them when we left. How do you all do this? It must cost quite a bit."

With a slight shrug of his elegant shoulders, he searched her face with an expression not unlike a laboratory researcher studying his specimen. His lips twitched. "You say the strangest things, Miss Standish. I am not sure what you are asking."

She shot him a dark look and stomped her foot...just a bit. "Oh, stop this silly act, *Bobby*. Y'all are driving me nuts. I feel like I've landed in a madhouse."

Apparently unimpressed by her righteous rage, he chuckled and murmured in a low voice. "I am beginning to feel the same way, Miss Standish."

"Mr. Chamberlain, can I help you?" A tall man who appeared to be in his early forties approached—his wheel hat, dark suit and bow tie marking him as a conductor. A thick dark mustache dominated his pale face. Blue eyes flickered to Ellie and then back to Robert. He moved with a balanced stride undeterred by the rocking of the train, coming to a halt in front of Ellie and Robert, his manner deferential but quietly authoritative.

"Yes, Conductor, Miss—"

"I can speak for myself. Listen, Mr...er..." With no encouragement from the conductor, she gulped and hurried on. "Listen, sir, somehow I've gotten myself onto this section of the train by accident. I don't know what happened. I went to sleep last night and when I woke up..." She paused, catching his perplexed eyes sliding toward Robert. "Excuse me, could you look at me and not Mr. Chamberlain, please? I'm talking." Ellie tilted her head back and eyed both tall men with irritation and a certain amount of trepidation as they exchanged a glance. What if she stood on tiptoe?

"Miss Standish...if you would allow me, perhaps I could explain to—"

"No, thanks, Robert. I've got this covered." She tossed the words over her shoulder and turned back to the conductor. "If you would just listen to me for a moment." She swallowed hard, her courage failing. Why did the man continue to look over her head to Robert? "What I'm trying to say is I'm in seat 31B... That's where I went to sleep last night. This morning, I woke up on his carriage." She jerked her head in Robert's direction. "I don't know how or why...and believe me, I *will* be seeing a doctor about this when I get back, but for right now, I'd just like to get back to my seat, get my purse and get myself organized." She gulped air and waited expectantly.

The conductor stared at her with troubled eyes and a grave expression.

"Miss...er...Standish, I am not sure what has occurred here. We do not in fact have a seat 31B." Could you be mistaken about the number?" She caught his veiled glance at her clothing. "Could you perhaps be traveling in tourist class or—forgive me—in immigrant class?"

Chapter Four

Although the dining car seemed warm, in fact too warm, Ellie broke out into a cold sweat. Her knees buckled slightly, and she would have slid to the floor had Robert not caught her elbow. She turned to him with a beseeching look.

"Robert, help me. Please don't continue to do this." She turned back to the conductor. "Are you part of this thing, as well?"

He raised a thick, dark eyebrow. "Thing, Miss Standish?"

She sighed and rubbed her forehead. What a nightmare!

"This period piece you all are doing." She heard the exhaustion in her voice.

"Miss Standish, please let me lead you to a table. I think you need something to eat or drink." Robert slid his hand from her elbow to the small of her back and guided her forward. The conductor stood to the side to let them pass. "Conductor, if you will allow us a few minutes..."

"Certainly, Mr. Chamberlain. Take as much time as you need." He pulled a large golden watch from his coat pocket and flicked it open. "We reach Wenatchee in forty minutes."

Ellie watched in bemusement. Robert propelled her forward like a small child. About a dozen men and women occupied most of the tables in the dining car—all of them in period costume of the late Victorian/early Edwardian era—the women in lovely high-collar lace shirtwaist blouses and decorative hats, the men in suits with vests, many of them sporting large mustaches. Ellie felt their stares as she and Robert moved through the car. She had obviously crashed someone's private Victorian party, but the wide-eyed look of astonishment on several faces seemed unduly...astonished.

They neared a small table at the opposite end of the

car, and Robert pulled out a chair for her. She sank into it gratefully, her knees continuing to buckle in an unpredictable way. At least he didn't have one of the ubiquitous mustaches!

"You know," she said with a shaky smile as she watched Robert take the chair across the table, "maybe I do need a little something to eat. I'm pretty sure my blood sugar must be dropping. I just can't seem to get my knees to stop wobbling."

His green eyes surveyed her with compassion. "Yes, I did wonder if you weren't feeling well. Tell me, Miss Standish, are you in the medical profession? A nurse, perhaps?"

Busily scanning the elegant white linen-covered table for something edible such as crackers, she looked up at his words.

"No, why do you ask?"

"I just thought perhaps...your references to blood sugar suggest a knowledge of medicine."

She chuckled and leaned back in her chair, surprisingly more relaxed now that she was out of public view.

"Oh, *Bobby*. How long are you going to continue this charade? You guys are a hoot! And if I weren't so tired or confused, I could appreciate it. But as it is, I'm starved and I'm exhausted."

To her satisfaction, he winced. "My dear Miss Standish, please do not call me by that childish name." He turned to signal for a steward. Samuel seemed to materialize out of nowhere.

"Samuel. There you are. We thought we had lost you."

"I'm sorry, Mr. Chamberlain. The conductor came when you did. I didn't have a chance to talk to him."

Ellie watched the exchange with interest. Robert certainly had a way about him, a sort of friendly yet distant lord-of-the-manor confidence that she found both irritating and intriguing. Of course, it was a performance, but still...

"We would like a menu, Samuel. Miss Standish needs some nourishment."

"How about you, Mr. Chamberlain?" Samuel

instantly whipped out a paper menu from a mysterious location behind his back and laid it in front of Ellie.

"Nothing for me, Samuel. We just had dinner, as you well know."

Ellie raised her eyes from the rather intriguing menu to see Robert watching her while he spoke to Samuel. She blushed at his direct gaze. Samuel melted away.

"Y-you're not eating?" she stammered. "Listen, I can eat by myself. You don't have to wait with me." She threw him a bright grin, as toothy as she could make it. "I'll just have a quick snack, snag that conductor and find my car."

"It is no trouble, Miss Standish. I think I should wait with you, to see if you feel unwell again."

Her face flamed again, and she dropped her eyes to the menu. As with most things that day, the menu proved to be another facet of her continuing nightmare in Victorian land.

"Does this really say *boiled leg of mutton*? Boy, you guys really went all out on this. I don't even know anyone who eats boiled leg of mutton. The prices are great, though." Ellie glanced up at Robert and pointed to the menu. "Seventy-five cents for the food." She shook her head and chuckled. "I can't imagine how they swung that price."

"I eat boiled leg of mutton, Miss Standish. Now, you know someone who does."

A quick glance revealed he maintained a straight face...and a handsome one, at that. He leaned back in his chair, his posture relaxed, green eyes watching her with amused interest. Ellie couldn't help but be flattered. Kyle never looked at her like that. She couldn't really understand why Robert did. She knew she looked a frump, but it hadn't mattered.

"Cute, Robert, really cute," Ellie chuckled. She set the menu aside. "Listen, I'm not all that hungry. I just need a snack. I think I'll just have some cheese and crackers. You know, a little protein."

Robert's lips twitched and he crinkled his brow. "Protein?"

"Yes, you know...protein. Cheese."

He nodded. "Ah, cheese. Are you sure you wouldn't like to have something more to eat? Some soup, perhaps,

31

something hot?"

She shook her head. "No, that will be enough." She craned her neck to see down the length of the car, aware some of the other diners continued to throw curious glances in their direction...especially the women. "Now, where did Samuel go?"

Without turning around, Robert raised his hand, and Samuel appeared. Ellie's eyes widened. How did he do that?

"Hey, Samuel. Okay, could I have some of this Edam cheese and some crackers?" She pointed to the menu.

Samuel's eyes widened, and he threw an inquiring look at Robert.

Ellie put a stop to that. She waved her hand. "Yoohoo, Samuel! Over here. Pay attention to me. This is *my* order. I'm paying for it—or I will when I find my purse."

"Yes, ma'am." Samuel dipped his head and hurried away. She followed his retreating back, perplexed by his actions. Then she brought her eyes back to Robert who watched her with a puzzled frown.

"You could be kinder to him, Miss Standish. He is only doing his job."

She glanced at Robert in surprise. *Her?* Was he serious? He wasn't laughing.

"I *am* kind to him. In fact, I feel kind of sorry for him that he has to play this weird subservient role in your program here."

"Program?" He cocked a dark eyebrow in her direction.

"Well, whatever you want to call it. I'm just tired of everyone looking at you when I talk to them. It's really very odd. Makes me feel like I'm living in the Dark Ages."

A corner of his mouth lifted slowly. "The Dark Ages?" His smile broadened. "Surely not, Miss Standish. It is the turn of the century. We are much more advanced and civilized than the *Dark Ages*."

"Oh yeah, the turn of the century. I forgot," she murmured with a sigh. Ellie planted her elbows on the table and rested her chin on her palms. She steeled herself to meet his eyes with a steady gaze.

"Okay, Robert, I'll play along. What year is it?"

Robert's amused gaze, which had fixed on her elbows on the table, returned to her face with a glint. "1901, Miss Standish. As I said, the turn of the century. And a fine year it is proving to be."

She sniffed and shook her head with a wry twist of her lips. "Mmmhmmm. Okay. And who is the President?"

His smile widened to an amused grin. He reached for a glass of water delivered by Samuel and took a deliberate sip before answering.

"William McKinley. And since we are *playing* at questions, I believe it must be my turn, Miss Standish."

Ellie narrowed her eyes and regarded him for a moment before crossing her arms and leaning back into her chair with a half smile.

"Okay, go ahead."

"What is your first name?" The sparkle in his green eyes robbed her of breath for a moment. Her heart bumped against her chest.

"Ellie," she murmured, suddenly shy at the unexpectedly intimate quality of such an ordinary question.

"Ellie," he repeated. The well-known name sounded suddenly fresh and desirable on his lips. "And does that stand for Eleanor?"

She inhaled deeply to bring oxygen back to her deprived brain, and she hugged herself tightly.

"No, just Ellie. It's just a name my hippie-dippy parents decided to give me."

"Hippie-dippy?" He shook his head with a wry smile. "And what part of the country are you from, Ellie? May I call you Ellie?"

"Oh yeah, sure. Ummm..." She was distracted by a sudden memory of the man who had sat next to her on the train yesterday...a similar question. Was it only yesterday? She remembered the color of his eyes...green.

"Ellie?" Robert repeated his question with an inquiring arch of an eyebrow. She met his questioning eyes...the same green.

She shook off the odd coincidence. "I'm sorry. What was the question?"

"Where are you from?"

"Oh, Chicago. Well, no, not really. I mean I live in

Chicago now. I've moved around a lot, though."

"I see. I have been to Chicago several times. Some of your expressions stupefy me. I do not believe I have heard them in Chicago, either. What do you mean by hippie-dippy parents?"

"Oh, so you're saying you haven't heard that expression, either, Robert?" She studied his face through narrowed eyes. His face registered genuine curiosity. Was it possible?

"Well, maybe you haven't. I'll give you that. But you have heard of hippies, right? The late sixties and early seventies? San Francisco? Woodstock?"

She watched various expressions cross his face, the most prominent being a look of confusion. "Well, certainly I've heard of San Francisco. In fact, I've been there. The sixties and seventies? The reconstruction era?"

She almost laughed, but she wouldn't give him the satisfaction.

"Robert, you have an American accent, but are you actually *from* the United States? Everyone knows about hippies...flower children." The train took a sudden lurch, and water sloshed from Ellie's glass. She was surprised the whole glass hadn't jumped off the table by now, with the uneven movements of these old-fashioned carriages.

He quirked a quizzical eyebrow in her direction.

"Well, unless you are referring to children who carry flowers in a wedding procession, I have no earthly idea what you are talking about. Please instruct me."

She opened her mouth to retort, but Samuel appeared with a silver tray. He set an elegant porcelain plate before Ellie with slices of Edam cheese and saltine crackers.

"Oh, thank you, thank you, Samuel. I'm starving."

Samuel nodded, threw a last glance at Robert and moved away.

Ellie sliced several small sections off the small block and laid them on the crackers.

"Are you sure you don't want some?"

"No, thank you. I am fine."

She bit into her snack and paused, her teeth seemingly hitting solid rock. With a self-conscious glance in Robert's direction, she pulled the food from the edge of her mouth and examined the cracker. While it looked like a saltine, she could see now that the small white square was thicker than a saltine. With another flushed look in Robert's direction, she bit into the cracker again. It gave way this time, and she ground it in her mouth.

With one bite of the hard cracker swallowed, she eyed the rest with misgiving. She reached for her water to help the food make its way to its final destination.

"Wow, those crackers are really hard." Hungry and unwilling to fight the food, she popped a slice of the salty cheese into her mouth.

"They used to be called hardtack. Haven't you ever eaten them before?"

"Hardtack?" She eyed the crackers again with suspicious eyes. "Hardtack? Are you serious? No wonder. I've never had hardtack before." Ellie picked up another cracker and attempted to nibble the edges.

"Don't they have hardtack in Chicago, Ellie?"

"Not that I'm aware of. At least not in this century."

"How interesting." He lowered his eyes for a moment while he ran his finger around the rim of his water glass. "Tell me, Ellie. Are you married?"

Ellie almost choked on the dry cracker and grabbed another gulp of water.

"Er, no, I'm not." She bit her lip. She hesitated to say the words *But I'm engaged*, and she didn't know why.

"No Mr. Standish?" He raised playful dark-lashed eyes to her face. She blushed.

"No Mr. Standish. How about you, Robert? Are you married?"

"No, I am currently not so fortunate."

Ellie chuckled at his odd speech pattern. "Never been married?"

"If I had ever been married, Ellie, I would still be wedded...to the same woman."

Her heart caught in her throat. He stared at her with a steady gaze, a half-smile playing on his lips. His words seemed so certain, so confident, so...permanent.

She cleared her throat. "Well, certainly. Of course. I just...well, you know, a lot of people are divorced these days. You never know. I...uh...I didn't mean to be rude."

"I did not take offense." His smile widened to a grin.

"I intend to marry only once, and I have not yet found the woman who could put up with me for the rest of her life." The twinkle returned to his eyes, but Ellie had no doubt about his firm stance.

"Mr. Chamberlain, Miss Standish. Is this a good time for me to interrupt? The train will be pulling into Wenatchee in a few minutes. I think we need to get Miss Standish sorted out at that time."

The conductor towered over the table, his wide stance preventing any need to brace himself against the rocking of the train.

Robert glanced up at him and turned to Ellie. "Do you feel better, Ellie? Have you eaten enough?"

Ellie nodded, having eaten only three slices of cheese. "Yes, I'm fine. I'll be glad to get back to my seat. I could use a nap." She gave Robert a small smile, hoping he wouldn't see the lie in her eyes—a lie that took her by surprise.

"Good. That is settled, then. I must return to my carriage to check on the ladies. They will be worried about my extended absence by now. It seems as if Mr..."

"Bingham, sir."

"It appears as if Mr. Bingham is going to assist you in whatever way you need." Robert gave her an encouraging smile, and turned to the conductor, who stood by silently.

"You will let me know if Miss Standish needs any further assistance, of course. My family and I are more than happy to see to anything she needs should her seat...ah...go missing."

Ellie rose slowly from the table and smiled with a slight shake of her head.

"You know, Robert, I'm beginning to think I woke up in another dimension...in a time warp. You're good, I'll give you that. I'll find my seat, if Mr. Bingham here points me the way."

She put out a hand. Robert looked at it for a moment, and then took it in his own warm grasp. She caught her breath.

"Thank you for everything, Robert. Again, it's been fun." Ellie reluctantly pulled her hand from his.

Robert tipped an invisible hat in her direction.

"As you say, Ellie, it has been fun. I will see you again." He turned away and strode down the length of the dining car, leaving Ellie to stare in his wake, temporarily robbed of breath, a delightful tingling in her hand.

"Miss Standish?"

She turned bemused eyes up to the solemn face of the tall conductor.

"Yes, Mr. Bingham?"

"Shall we?" He indicated a doorway at the nearest end of the train.

"Oh, but I have to pay for my meal." Her face burned. "Except I have to find my purse first."

"Of course. We can see to that shortly."

"Oh, okay." Ellie staggered and grabbed the table as the train lurched to a stop. Mr. Bingham reached out to steady her.

"Thanks."

He pulled his watch out of his pocket and regarded it for a moment. "It seems we have arrived. We should be here for thirty minutes. I think I had better take you down to the tourist cars to see if you recognize your seat."

"Oh, great!"

"I wonder if you could wait here for me until I return. Now that we have arrived, I have one or two duties to attend to in the station and then I can return for you. I shouldn't be more than a few moments at the most."

Ellie scanned the room, now empty of diners. Stewards moved about, cleaning tables and setting out new dinnerware.

"Can't I wait outside the car? I could use some fresh air and it looks like they're pretty busy cleaning up in here."

He barely glanced at the busy stewards. "I do not like to leave you alone outside. I think it would be better if you were to wait here."

She shrugged and sank back into her seat, wondering if he worried she would disappear without paying her bill or providing proof of her train fare. With a tip of his wheel cap, he consulted his watch again and walked out the door.

Ellie strained to see out the windows, but dust impeded her view. She threw another glance at the stewards, who paused occasionally to stare at her. Feeling as if she'd worn out her welcome, she jumped up and pushed open the door with the intention of waiting for the conductor outside.

She stepped out onto the landing and was immediately assaulted by the thick smell of coal. To her surprise, the car appeared to connect to another historical carriage. How many of them were there, she wondered.

A peek through the glass of the door to the left revealed a dusty field of harvested corn. She turned to the right and opened the door, gingerly descending the old iron stairs down to gravel. The train depot caught her eye first, a small old-fashioned wooden structure with a boardwalk in front. Several people rested on benches or milled about stretching their legs.

She shook her head with a sigh. They too wore costumes, mostly as she had seen in the dining car, but a few men who leaned against walls sported ragged felt hats, western-style flannel shirts, and thick dungarees that seemed the worse for wear. With a deepening sense of the surreal, she noticed a tall man, obviously Native American, with unkempt long dark hair, wearing a ragged flannel shirt and dark, baggy trousers. He was standing at the edge of the platform with a short, stout woman half hidden by the grubby blanket that covered her frame, a baby's face peeping out from her arms. The man raised his hand occasionally, bringing it to his mouth in a universal gesture requesting food. The strolling passersby ignored him.

An overwhelming atmosphere of dry dust permeated the air, and Ellie sneezed vigorously. Nothing at the minuscule station seemed remotely modern. The weathered wood and grimy windows of the building gave way to the warped boardwalk that led across a dirt road toward the gravel around the train tracks. She moved away from the train to investigate further. As she did so, she looked to her right and saw Robert on the ground assisting the ladies of his party down. He seemed not to see her, and that was fine with Ellie.

What she saw next took her breath away...perhaps even her sanity. She turned around to see twenty or so old-fashioned carriages just like hers, stretching away toward the front of the train. Gone were the modern gleaming silver cars she'd boarded in Chicago. Every single car seemed to have come straight out of a vintage railroad photograph.

Ellie's knees began to shake as she stood in the middle of the tracks staring helplessly at the train. She broke out into a cold sweat; her mouth tasted of a nasty mixture of pungent coal, dry dust and bitter bile. A wave of nausea overtook her, and she turned toward the station to beg someone to save her from the nightmare. No sounds came from her frozen throat. The station blurred and grew suddenly dark.

Chapter Five

"Ellie. Ellie." A familiar masculine voice penetrated her consciousness. She rubbed her face against the warm hand touching her cheek. "Miss Standish, wake up." Not Miss Standish again, she thought with confused dismay. Heavy eyelids refused to open, and she stopped fighting them for a moment as she listened to the hazy murmur of the voices in her dream.

"Robert, come away. Give the girl some air. Is there a physician on this infernal train?"

"No, Grandmother. I have already made inquiries."

"Do you think she is malnourished, Robert? She seemed so strange, so confused...almost delirious."

"No, Melinda, I do not think she is malnourished. She certainly looks well fed."

Ellie forced her eyes open to find Robert's concerned green eyes close to her face as he bent over her.

"Is that a fat joke?" Her parched throat thickened her voice.

Robert startled and blinked. "Ellie...Miss Standish, are you all right?" He withdrew his hand and straightened slowly. "A *fat* joke? Good gravy! Certainly not!"

Melinda hovered behind him, her smooth white brow knitted above troubled blue eyes. Ellie tried to sit up.

"Stay there, Miss Standish, until we are sure you are feeling better."

"I'm fine, Robert. I need to sit up. I feel queasy."

"Very well, madam. Here." Robert helped her into a sitting position. She recognized her original bench seat, which was fortunately long enough for her to recline on. Amy and several of the other young women peered around the corner with anxious faces. Mrs. Chamberlain sat on the bench opposite and stared at her with a frown.

"Here, Robert, a glass of water."

"Excellent, Melinda. Thank you." He handed the

glass to Ellie, who took a drink. She wrinkled her nose at the metallic taste but obediently drank a few sips. Anything to rid her mouth and throat of the dust.

The dust...

She looked up at Robert. "How did I get back on board?" A sudden lurch of the carriage jerked her toward reality, and she realized the train had been rumbling along the tracks since she'd been conscious. She bolted upright and gasped. "The train is moving, isn't it?"

"Robert picked you up off the ground like a limp rag doll and brought you back onto the train. You've been unconscious...or asleep, for some time." Mrs. Chamberlain folded pale hands on the black silk of her lap and surveyed Ellie with sharp blue eyes.

"We pulled out of Wenatchee almost a half hour ago, Ellie." The quiet sympathy in Robert's voice threatened to break down her reserves. "I'm sorry we were not able to locate your seat. We thought it best to bring you back on board."

Ellie stared at him with wide eyes. His well-groomed clothes...so vintage...so new! She looked past him to Mrs. Chamberlain. Impossible to think she could ever have worn a polyester leisure suit. And Melinda? A short, frisky platinum blonde color and cut to her gorgeous hair? Never!

"Ellie?"

Robert's insistent voice brought her back to a nightmare come true. The train...her seat. Where did they go? She returned her stricken gaze to his face. The kindly inquisitive tilt of his head as he looked at her broke the floodgates

"I-I'm lost. I don't know where I am," she wailed before she burst into tears, pulled her knees to her chest and buried her face in her hands. She hadn't known terror like this since she was a child waking up from a nightmare. Her mother would come to her then, sit on the bed beside her and tell her it was only a bad dream...that it would go away. And it always did...then.

But her mother didn't come this time. Robert did.

"Don't cry, Ellie. I am going to help you find your way home, wherever that is. Don't cry. Everything is going to be all right." Robert's soothing voice spoke near her ear.

He'd lowered himself to one knee and leaned against the bench beside her. She turned a water-stained face to him, wishing he would take her in his arms as her mother once had.

"I hope you *can* help me, Robert. I'm done pretending I have a clue. I'm so confused. I don't know where my seat is anymore. I don't know where I am."

"What is she going on about, Robert? Ellie— Is that her name? Ellie, what do you mean, you are lost? Melinda, give her that blanket there to cover her legs. No well-bred woman sits that way."

In a daze, Ellie watched Melinda spring into action and pick up a dark blue wool blanket which she carefully spread over Ellie's hunched legs.

"Give her some time, Grandmother. She seems to have had quite a shock. This is hardly the time to worry about proper behavior."

"Hmmppfff. I have had a shock or two in my time, Robert, and I never forgot my manners."

Luckily, Ellie's view of Mrs. Chamberlain was blocked by Robert's face...his handsome face.

"Grandmother, why don't you and Melinda return to the observation lounge? I'd like to talk to Miss Standish in private."

Robert kept a searching gaze on Ellie's face while he spoke over his shoulder.

"Well, I hope you are able to make some sense of what she says. Mind you keep that blanket on her. She probably needs the warmth."

Robert rose to his full height and extended his arm to the older woman to help her rise. She peered around him one more time to examine Ellie before he led her to Melinda, who took her arm and retreated to the rear of the car.

A swell of female voices greeted their return, and then settled into a hum of questions and answers.

Robert turned back to Ellie, allowing his gaze to rest momentarily on the open bench beside her before he tightened his lips and moved to take a seat on the opposite bench. Ellie would have welcomed his nearness— in fact, she craved his very real presence in a world gone mad.

"You can sit here, Robert."

"It would not be proper, Ellie."

"Oh." Her face burned, and she pulled the soft woolen blanket toward her cheeks. She threw him a quick glance before she lowered her eyes to study the threads of the blanket.

"Ellie." The gravity in his quiet voice terrified her. She didn't want him to talk. Anything he had to say would be bad news. She was certain of it.

"Yes?" She raised reluctant eyes to his face. A muscle flexed in his jaw. His dark-lashed eyes watched her with a mixture of curiosity and concern. She burst into babble.

"I know you think I'm crazy, Robert. I can't even find my train, the one I boarded yesterday in Chicago. You know, the bright shining modern train that we all know and love. That one?"

He watched her patiently, his legs crossed elegantly, hands clasped in his lap.

Ellie hardly stopped for breath before she began again with an unladylike snort. "Of course, I think you guys are a bit whacked out myself. Or at least, I did...until I discovered I've lost my train. It's not possible for me to fall asleep and wake up on another train...especially a vintage one."

She paused for a gulp of air. Robert tilted his head in that charming way, a hint of a smile on his face.

"I mean it's really not possible, unless I'm still dreaming. And I could be dreaming, Robert. Don't think I haven't thought about that. For all I know, I could be having a conversation with a dream. Do you know what I mean?"

She ended on a winded note with a quick glance in Robert's direction. To her surprise, instead of responding, he rose and walked into the observation lounge, returning in seconds with a newspaper in his hands. He laid the paper on his bench and sat back down.

"Ellie." He began again in that same serious note that boded no good for her. "What year is it?"

Ellie's eyebrows shot up. She didn't know what she had expected, but that question wasn't it. She told him the current date.

Robert's eye's widened for a second and then

narrowed. It seemed as if he held his breath for a moment and then released it with a hiss. Propping his arms on his knees, he leaned forward intently as if to say something. Then he straightened abruptly and his eyes fell to the paper at his side.

Ellie watched his dark bent head nervously. What was he thinking?

With a slight shake of his head and a sigh, he picked up the paper and stared hard at it, passing it from one hand to the other.

"I don't think so, Ellie."

"You don't think what?"

"I wonder if you could be ill, as Melinda suggested. Have you been eating well? Had a recent illness, a bout with fever?"

Ellie kept her eye on the hands that handled the paper. What was it about that paper that worried him so much? She shook her head.

"No, I don't think so. I haven't been sick."

He opened the newspaper and handed it to her. She pulled her hands out from under the blanket and took it with an uncertain look in his direction. At first glance, the paper resembled a local free weekly such as one might find at the entrance to the grocery store. The uneven print caught her eye, garish and old-fashioned, as if it had been typed on a manual typewriter.

The bright, bold title caught her eye: *The Seattle Weekly*. Vivid headlines read "MOUNT BAKER PUFFS AGAIN." Ellie glanced at Robert curiously. He gave her an encouraging nod.

"What do you want me to look at?" She turned a page. The paper felt coarse, unlike the smooth newsprint from her local Chicago newspaper.

"The date, Ellie. Look at the date."

Ellie returned to the front page and searched above the oversized headlines for the date. She found it in the middle, the print italicized and difficult to read.

April 20, 1901. She mouthed the words silently. Nineteen hundred and one. That would be about right. The late Victorian/early Edwardian era. The year of Queen Victoria's death.

She turned to Robert, who had moved to the edge of

his seat.

"Do you see the date, Ellie?"

"Yes, April 20, 1901." She held up the paper and smiled wanly. "I assume this is part of your reenactment."

"Ellie, this is no reenactment. We do not prance about in Napoleonic costumes pretending to relive glorious days of the past." He pushed himself back against his bench and crossed his arms, directing a frank stare in her direction.

"So, what are you trying to say?" Ellie swallowed hard. Black dots swam before her eyes.

"I think you know what I'm trying to say. I believe you are being deliberately obtuse."

"I am not. I haven't got the faintest idea what you're talking about," she retorted hotly. Of course she did, but the reality just seemed too bizarre to comprehend.

Robert tightened his lips and eyed her speculatively. He leaned forward again.

"Have you ever read H. G. Wells?"

"Yes. Don't even try that, Robert." Ellie shook her head, a warning note in her voice.

"Have you read his book called *The Time Machine?*"

"Read it, watched the movie, loved it." She stared at Robert with narrowed eyes. She wasn't going to allow what would surely follow.

"I don't know about this *moovee* you mention, but you've read about his concept of time travel, then?"

"It's fiction, Robert. Time travel doesn't exist, as far as we know. Not even in the twenty-first century."

"That is my point, Ellie. This is not the twenty-first century. It is April 25, 1901." He crossed his arms again and regarded her with a strange light in his green eyes. "Now, either you *are* delirious as Melinda suggested, or..." He eyed her sympathetically. "Or..."

"Or I've traveled back in time?" She clapped a hand over her mouth to stifle a hysterical giggle. "Are those my only options?"

"Do you have an explanation for your appearance here...in your strange costume? Where is this seat you say you've lost?"

"*My* costume!" She ran her eyes up and down his handsome figure. "How about I fell asleep and somehow

45

accidentally walked off my own train in the middle of the night and walked into your historical party here?" Ellie stared at him, her belligerence betrayed by the fright in her eyes.

Robert's lips twitched. "Ellie," he murmured. "Do you really think that's likely?"

"There's a third alternative, Robert. One that makes more and more sense, now that I think about it."

"And what is that, my dear Miss Standish?"

"Well, Mr. Chamberlain, the other alternative is that this is all just a dream." She dropped the edge of the blanket and raised her hands expansively to encompass the train.

Robert's eyes crinkled when he laughed, and he shook his head patiently. "That is not possible, Ellie. It is simply impossible. I am real. I am no dream."

Having found an answer she could live with, Ellie prepared to defend it like a faithful follower. She relaxed her grip on her knees and rested her head against the high back of the velvet bench with a self-satisfied nod.

"How would you know this isn't a dream?"

"Well, I'm certain I would know. How could I not know?" Robert's steady gaze faltered. He stared down at the ground for a brief second before returning his gaze to Ellie's face. His voice was grave. He shook his head again. "No, this is not a dream, Ellie."

Ellie gave him a serene smile. All was right with the world at last.

"You would never know, Robert. Besides, this is *my* dream, but I'll tell you what I'm prepared to do." She pushed the blanket away, swung her legs over the edge of the seat and leaned forward. "I'm prepared to let you choreograph the dream, as it seems you've already been doing. I'll just sit back and let the dream take its course. How about that?"

She crossed her arms and leaned back against the seat once again, watching him from under veiled lashes. A myriad of emotions crossed his face—surprise, disbelief, a flash of something soft she did not recognize, and finally amusement.

Robert drew in breath to speak, and then closed his mouth. He turned away to stare at nothing in particular for just a moment. When he returned his gaze to her face, the twinkle sparkled in his eyes.

"So, you are saying that you are putting yourself in my hands in this dream of yours. Is that correct, Miss Standish?"

Suddenly full of the confidence only a dream could give her, she gave him a half-smile and a benign nod.

"Yes, Mr. Chamberlain, do with me what you will." Ellie grinned. "Within reason, of course."

Robert's dark eyebrows shot up for a moment before he responded.

"Excellent. I am prepared for the challenge of...er...choreographing your dream, then. Since your...em...dream has left you with no seat at your disposal and no visible income, you will come to my house, where my grandmother and sister reside, to stay with us...until you...em...wake up."

Ellie wasn't sure about the nature of dreams, but this one seemed to be taking a turn for the better. She took a deep breath.

"Sure, Robert. That sounds fine. I warn you, though. If you turn into some sort of murderer or monster, I'll do my best to wake up."

Robert's green eyes softened. "I am no monster, Ellie. I promise you that."

Ellie reached out to shake his hand. Robert stared at her hand for a moment and took it in his own. She gave it a good tug.

"Deal."

"Deal," he murmured, making no move to release her hand. She pulled away from his warmth reluctantly and leaned back against her seat.

"So, what's the plan?" she asked with interest.

Robert threw back his head and laughed—a hearty, happy sound that charmed her with its utter masculinity.

"You certainly are an enigma, Ellie. I think I had better let the ladies know you will be staying with us. There will be some concerns from Grandmother, no doubt. I suspect Melinda will be delighted to have such an...unusual houseguest."

Ellie grinned.

"I'm looking forward to the stay, Robert. I always did

47

want to know what life was like at the turn of the century."

"You promise to be quite an adventure, my dear Miss Standish." The sparkling challenge in Robert's eyes shook her bravado for a moment, but she recovered.

He rose slowly and gazed down at her briefly.

"Just remember, Ellie. It is my belief that you have traveled back in time, although I do not know why."

Ellie stared into the emerald depths of his eyes, afraid to lose herself in them.

"And *I* think this is all just a dream, Robert. One that could end at any moment."

His eyes darkened, and he reached down to trace the line of her left cheek with his index finger before straightening.

"Let us hope not...not too soon." He cleared his throat and ran a finger along the inside of his high collar. "I think you had better wait here until the questions are out of the way. You might find my grandmother... er...outspoken." He grinned.

"I noticed," Ellie murmured with a twitch of her lips.

He chuckled and moved away.

Ellie pulled her feet back up onto the seat and stretched out with the blanket, suddenly weary. Did people feel tired in dreams? Did they sleep? That seemed redundant. Had she ever even boarded the train in Chicago? When did the dream begin? She swallowed hard against a sudden knot in her throat. When would it end? Please, not too soon, she thought drowsily. Not too soon.

Chapter Six

"Ellie? Ellie, wake up." A gentle hand shook Ellie's shoulder. She awakened to her dream. Robert bent over her, his face close to hers. Melinda hovered behind, trying to peer over his shoulder.

"Robert, you're still here. I feel like I'm dreaming within a dream." She rubbed her eyes and attempted to sit up.

He threw a quick glance over his shoulder at Melinda and put a cautionary finger to his lips.

"And you are still here as well, Miss Standish. Melinda and my grandmother are looking forward to your visit with us."

Ellie's eyes shot open, and she focused on the warning message in Robert's eyes.

"Oh, my visit. Yes, thank you very much." Uncertain what he had told them, she faltered. "I-I look forward to staying with your family." She exchanged a quick conspiratorial glance with Robert who nodded and straightened.

"Well, we were wondering if you wanted to have a light supper with us. It will be served here in the observation car." Robert pulled out a lovely gold watch from a pocket in his gray vest. "We will arrive in Seattle in approximately two hours, at 11:30 p.m."

Her stomach growled at the thought of food, and she bobbed her head enthusiastically.

"Yes, I'd love to eat. How long have I been asleep?"

"About five hours, Miss Standish. You must have been exhausted." Melinda had finally managed to get around Robert to peer at Ellie.

Ellie's eyes flew to Robert's face.

"Five hours? I-I'm lucky I managed to wake up at all. Why aren't we in Seattle yet? How long is the trip from Wenatchee?"

Robert gave a short laugh, which did not reach his

49

eyes.

"I wasn't certain if you *were* going to wake up. You seemed dead to the world. The journey is nine hours."

"He's been very worried, Miss Standish," Melinda offered. "He's been back here about twenty times, checking on you as you continued to sleep. We told him you probably just needed some rest and to leave you alone, but Robert insisted he must check your breathing."

Ellie's face flamed and she found it hard to meet Robert's eyes.

"Shall we dine then, Miss Standish?" He held out an elegant arm, and Ellie rose to take it self-consciously. He led her toward the back of the carriage with Melinda following closely behind.

Soft lights now glowed overhead in brass and tulip chandeliers and cast a golden radiance over the teak walls and red velvet furnishings. Shades, pulled low against the night sky, lent the carriage an intimate atmosphere.

All the women turned curious eyes on Ellie once again, and she gave them a pleasant smile and sank into the chair Robert indicated. She did not miss the speculative eyes that studied both Robert and her, but she chose to ignore them.

Several of the younger women had removed their hats, revealing hairstyles similar to Melinda's—the upswept Gibson—albeit with a few limp, dangling curls and wayward wisps from the long traveling day. Ellie put a hand to her own curly brown hair to see how much of it had escaped her braid. Some tendrils hung around her face, and she stuck them behind her ears, though they instantly popped forward once again.

Samuel served from a tray of odd-looking food. Ellie thought she recognized slices of roast beef and ham, but the rest of the food was unfamiliar to her.

Robert took a vacant seat across the room next to his grandmother, who eyed Ellie with an inscrutable expression. Luckily, Samuel distracted her attention by handing the older woman a plate.

Samuel crossed the room to approach Ellie.

"What would you like to eat, miss?" He stood aside to let her study the food on the large silver tray in the middle of the room.

Ellie shook her head with dismay.

"Gosh, I don't know. So much meat. Do you have anything that isn't meat?"

Samuel's eyes widened. "Pardon, miss?"

"I'm a vegetarian." Ellie wrinkled her nose and gave Samuel a sheepish grin. "You know, I don't eat meat? Do you have a baked potato or something?"

"Robert, do go over and see what you can do to help Miss Standish. She seems to be having trouble communicating." Mrs. Chamberlain's voice rang out, bringing all eyes back to Ellie...again.

Robert rose and crossed the narrow space between them.

"Is something wrong, Samuel?"

"Sir, I'm afraid...I don't know what she wants." Samuel's eyes flickered nervously. Ellie hated to make him ill at ease. If she had truly awakened at the turn of the century...before the civil rights movement and lack of union representation, his subservient behavior made a great deal of sense. The man was afraid of losing his job at the whim of a cantankerous passenger.

"It's no problem, Robert. I'm afraid I'm giving Samuel a hard time. I don't eat meat, so I'm trying to figure out how I'm going to avoid starving to death while I'm here."

Robert blinked and drew his brows together. He turned to Samuel.

"Please wait on my sister and her guests, Samuel. I must consult with Miss Standish for a moment."

He held out his arm for Ellie, and she sighed and rose to take it, knowing all eyes continued to stare at her. Robert led her a few feet away, out of hearing, toward the front of the carriage.

"A vegetarian, is it?" The irresistible twitch of his lips returned, and Ellie stared helplessly at the deep dimples in his cheeks.

She nodded mutely.

"Well, since this is your *dream*, can't you just change that? I fear you'll become very hungry if you don't eat."

Ellie shook her head. "No, I don't think I can change it. Besides, we decided that you would *choreograph* the dream." She crossed her arms. "I'm just along for the ride."

He fixed her with a challenging eye.

"Very well, then. I command you to eat meat."

Ellie shook her head with exasperation and suppressed a gurgle of laughter.

"Ummm...no, Robert. I don't respond to commands, and I'm not going to eat meat...not even in my dream. Then it would become a nightmare."

He tightened his lips and leaned close to her face.

"So, I am to be the director of this dream, but am powerless, is that correct?"

Ellie smirked. "Well, I don't know how it's going to work, Robert. This *is* the first time I've been in this situation. I'm pretty sure *I'm* not in control of the dream, or I'd be lying on a sunny beach somewhere in a tropical paradise."

"Alone?" He quirked a teasing eyebrow.

"Most definitely not!" She waggled her brows suggestively.

Robert threw back his head and laughed, and Ellie responded with some nervous giggles of her own. She refused to turn around, knowing everyone was watching. When would they stop staring?

"If I could control the dream, Robert, I'd make everyone stop staring at me." She wiped tears of laughter from her eyes.

He caught his breath and looked past her to the room beyond.

"I'm afraid they will be watching for a while. Most of these young ladies are friends of Melinda. We took a trip to Spokane to celebrate her eighteenth birthday...a long and arduous journey which I'm not likely to repeat any time soon."

Ellie glanced over her shoulder. Most of the women had returned their attention to their food. She caught Constance staring at her...at Robert.

"Well, Ellie, what do you eat?"

"I think I'll just have some bread and cheese for now. I can't bear to see the worry in Samuel's eyes."

Robert nodded. "The working classes are at the whim and mercy of their employers. The system is changing, but it will take time. You and I must have a long discussion about the future. In the meantime, let us return to find some food for you to eat. I must remember to instruct our cook to prepare dishes of vegetables for you."

"Thanks, Robert. I hate to be so much trouble, but I can't seem to avoid it."

"Trouble, indeed," Robert laughed softly. "I think I can manage to cope."

Ellie glanced at him in confusion for a moment before she turned away. She faltered when she felt his hand on the small of her back.

If she were really in control of the dream, she and Robert would... She quashed the thought.

Kyle! Her dreams would never hurt him. He would never know.

****

Dinner over and most of the women dozing in their chairs, Robert stared at the fascinating creature that was Ellie. She rested her shining brown head of hair against the velvet drapes in the corner of the observation carriage, her feet crossed at the ankles in front of her like a child, her full-lipped mouth slightly parted, dark lashes against her pale cheeks.

He had no doubt that Ellie had magically descended on them for a reason, and he hoped he was that reason. That she'd given herself over to him in need was a sign, and he was honored to have the care of the strange woman who had traveled through time. Though Ellie believed she was in a dream, Robert knew different. Ellie had come for him. She was the woman for whom he'd waited all these years.

He turned to look at his grandmother, who gently snored next to him. He hated to shock the older woman, and he hoped her heart could survive the news, but he was determined to have Ellie for his own...if she stayed. He did not yet understand how she'd ended up in his time, but he fervently hoped she would stay. He couldn't wait to discover what wondrous things she would reveal about life in the twenty-first century.

When she had fainted and fallen to the ground at the train depot, his heart had seized and he'd raced to her side, picking her up tenderly and brushing the dust from her soft brown hair. He had brushed off Mr. Bingham's entreaties to leave her to the care of the stationmaster.

53

Impossible. He might never have seen her again. Ellie was no *immigrant* in the original sense of the word. She came from another place, that seemed certain, but that place was the future, and she had come to him.

He tilted his head and regarded her with a frown. Why didn't she realize that? He knew it was the truth. How would he convince her?

He blinked and felt warmth rush to his face when he realized Ellie had opened her eyes to catch him staring at her. She straightened in her chair and flashed him a shaky smile.

Poor girl! So lost. He knew an overwhelming desire to cross the carriage and settle into a chair beside her, to hold her hand and study the hazel mix of her eyes. But there was no chair nearby, and he understood the need to move slowly. He did not want to frighten her away...back in time...or back into her dream.

"She is an interesting woman, isn't she, Robert?" Constance, apparently having followed his eyes, whispered next to him.

He turned to her with a start and looked back at Ellie, who studiously smoothed wrinkles from her skirt.

"Yes, she is, Constance. Poor thing. She seems so lost. I feel compelled to assist."

"Why, Robert, if I may ask? She *is* a stranger. What drove you to bring her back to the carriage when the conductor offered to see to her?"

Robert dragged his eyes from Ellie. Her nonchalant picking at her skirt suggested she knew she was the subject of discussion. He looked at Constance. "I cannot explain it. I thought she would be safer with us. I do not think she is from the *immigrant* car, nor do I think she is mentally unstable. I intend to bring her to the house and see if she recovers her..."

"Wits?" Constance smiled.

"Constance," Robert reproved. He bit his tongue against an acerbic retort. "Recovers her bearings."

"Oh, I see," she murmured. "Well, take care, Robert."

Robert turned startled eyes to her. "Careful of what, Constance?"

"Yourself." She smiled, but her eyes were veiled.

"Nonsense, Constance." He grinned, hoping to throw

her off the scent. Was he that obvious?

****

The train pulled into Seattle's Union Station at midnight. Having slept for the past two hours, Melinda and her friends quickly tidied their hair, donned their hats and threw on jackets and shawls.

Robert stood and helped his grandmother to her feet. He signaled for Melanie to assist the exhausted and pale woman while he crossed the room and bent his head near Ellie.

"Just follow me."

Ellie nodded, fascinated by the hustle and bustle accompanying the arrival of the train. As Robert moved away to supervise their disembarkation in an orderly fashion, she caught Constance's eye again from across the room. For the past few hours, the dark-haired beauty had sat next to Robert, conversing with him in low tones...much to Ellie's chagrin. The intimacy of their conversation suggested a close relationship.

Had Robert forgotten to mention that he had a girlfriend...a lady love or whatever they called them in 1901? Had she bothered to ask? Could she awaken from this dream if it became unbearable?

"Ladies, shall we?" Robert took the lead and descended the steps, followed by his grandmother and Melinda. The young women followed, and Constance brought up the rear. Ellie lingered a moment to study the Victorian carriage one last time, committing its details to memory. Constance paused at the door.

"Miss Standish, are you coming?"

Ellie turned bemused eyes on her.

"Yes, I am. I'm right behind you."

Constance gave Ellie a friendly smile and descended the steps. Ellie hesitated at the top of the stairs for a moment, gripping the handrail tightly. The last time she'd stepped off this train, she had passed out. What would happen this time?

Robert's hand reached for hers.

"Come with me, Ellie. Stay close. I have a lot of women to see to, and I cannot lose you."

Ellie's heart jumped to her throat at his words. She took the last step and fell into line with the women of his

55

group. Robert gave her hand a quick squeeze before he let it go and moved to the front of the group to direct the unloading of luggage and the arrival of carriages.

Carriages? Ellie's eyes, nose and ears widened to the sensory overload of Seattle at the turn of the century. The smell of coal permeated the thick air of the bustling train station. The overheated locomotive hissed as leftover steam billowed onto the tracks. Conductors strode briskly along the wooden platform, barking out orders to porters who unloaded baggage and reloaded it onto wagons behind depressed-looking mules whose heads hung low. Several carriages awaited the exhausted arrivals, with restless horses that pawed the dirt road and whinnied.

"Melinda, please take Grandmother and Ellie to our carriage. You see Jimmy just over there?" He nodded in the direction of a large, black, hooded carriage. "I need to see your friends to their carriages. I trust you said your goodbyes."

Melinda hadn't, it seemed, for the young women gathered around her with squeals of gratitude and coos of promised visits in the coming days. Ellie stood to the side, watching everything as if she were in a dream...which of course she was. Finally, Robert was able to hand his grandmother off to Melinda and escort the rest of the young women to several waiting carriages. Further loud squeals of delight from inside the carriages proclaimed the welcome of family members.

"What a wonderful birthday party!" Melinda sighed, tucking her arm into her grandmother's.

"Come along, Melinda. Let's make our way to the carriage. I have been standing too long on these old legs. Miss Standish, if you please."

Ellie obediently moved forward in their wake, but she hesitated when she saw Constance standing alone under an ornate gas streetlamp. Ellie was just about to see if Constance needed a ride when she saw Robert move toward the dark-haired beauty. He bent his head, now covered with a dashing derby, near hers and she laughed brightly. Ellie cringed as Constance laid one dark-gloved hand on Robert's arm and accompanied him toward a waiting carriage. Was he going to take her home?

"Miss Standish, are you coming?"

Ellie barely heard Melinda's polite inquiry as she watched the handsome couple through narrowed eyes. If this was a dream, then she might be able to wish Constance somewhere else. Nothing dreadful...just gone.

Ellie squeezed her eyes shut and wished. Go away, Constance. Go away on a vacation to a wonderful spa or something and meet some nice man. Ellie's eyes shot open at the sound of the soft thud of horses' hooves and jingling harnesses.

"Miss Standish, do you intend to stand out there all night? What on earth are you doing?"

Ellie opened her mouth to answer Mrs. Chamberlain but stilled as she watched Robert materialize out of the darkness and walk toward her, his hand outstretched in her direction.

She put her hand in his and tilted her head back to search his eyes. His dimples deepened with his grin.

"Why haven't you climbed aboard the carriage? Won't my grandmother let you on?"

"Nonsense, Robert. The girl has been standing there gawking at who knows what."

Robert handed Ellie up into the carriage. She marveled at the sturdiness of the iron steps and soft comfort of the velvet seat as she slid in across from Melinda and her grandmother. Robert climbed in beside her, ducking low to avoid hitting his hat on the carriage roof.

The driver raised the steps, and within moments the carriage pulled forward with a jerk, to the sound of snorting horses and creaking wheels.

Ellie turned to glance out of the window and saw the "immigrant class," finally released from their cars, shuffling along the boardwalk. For the most part, they seemed poor and downtrodden. No bright white shirtwaists or clean silk skirts for the women. No well-tailored dark suits and highly polished shoes for the men. Many of the women covered themselves and their children with thick shawls, while the men wore various styles of ill-fitting thick coats. The travelers looked exhausted as they trudged along, dragging suitcases and hauling bulging cloth sacks. The once-helpful porters stood by and leaned on walls, offering no assistance to the tired mass.

Ellie watched with a frown as some people moved toward large open-air wagons while others made their way down the street on foot, tired children clinging to skirts and huddling close. The group seemed strangely hushed; only the occasional fretful cry of a baby broke the loud silence. She watched and wondered about their lives until she could see them no more.

In general, Seattle seemed much quieter at night in 1901 than in modern day. It bore little resemblance to the bustling city she'd enjoyed visiting on occasion. No bright streetlights shone down from above to show the way, no traffic signals blinked orange in the intersections, no testy car horns blared.

"Robert, now that we are alone and you've had time to think, I was wondering what your plans for Miss...ah...Standish are?"

Ellie dragged her eyes and ears away from the eerily dark and silent city to look at Robert. He glanced at her with a reassuring smile.

"I'm not sure, Grandmother. I think that is something Miss Standish and I will discuss at a more convenient time...and certainly in private."

"I see," his grandmother said in an icy tone. "And what am I to make of that?"

"Mrs. Chamberlain, I'm just staying for—"

"No need, Ellie. Grandmother welcomes you as our guest...as *my* guest. Forgive her. She is tired from the journey, I suspect."

Ellie squirmed as she watched and heard the conflict between the two of them. By the soft yellow light of the interior coach lamp, Ellie saw Mrs. Chamberlain gaze at her grandson for a moment with an unreadable expression. The older woman closed her eyes for a brief second and ran a hand lightly across her pale forehead. When she opened her eyes, she inclined her head in Robert's direction.

"Of course, you are right, Robert. I apologize if I seem rude, Miss Standish. I am weary, and I have forgotten my manners. Naturally, any guest of Robert's is welcome in his home."

"Well, I certainly look forward to your visit, Miss Standish...Ellie. May I call you Ellie?" Melinda leaned forward, seemingly full of energy even at this late hour.

"Uh...sure, Melinda. Thank you."

"Wonderful!"

Ellie grinned at Melinda's infectious goodwill. Before she could respond to Mrs. Chamberlain, the older woman closed her eyes and leaned her head back, to all intents and purposes unavailable for communication.

She looked up at Robert beside her to find him watching her with half-closed eyes.

"Are you tired?" she asked. The rocking of the carriage made her eyes heavy, as well.

"I am, a little. It's been a long journey. Two days to Spokane and two days to return."

"Two days? Of course, that seems correct, but I can't imagine." She glanced at Melinda, now dozing next to her grandmother, and lowered her voice, cupping her mouth. "It's only about seven hours by train now."

Robert's eyebrows shot up. "It does not seem possible." He shook his head slowly.

Ellie had an almost overwhelming urge to take off his derby and lower his sleepy-looking head to her lap, but she managed to resist the compulsion. Not only would she shock Melinda and Mrs. Chamberlain with such a bold move, a struggle might possibly ensue if Robert bucked her plans and decided to remain upright. She stifled a chuckle at the image of the awkward moment.

"What makes you laugh, Ellie?" Her heart fluttered at the intimate note in his voice. She blushed at the thought of telling him why she laughed.

"I can't say, Mr. Chamberlain." She took a deep breath and turned to stare out the window into the darkness, but his warm, strong fingers guided her chin back toward him.

He tilted her face towards his, forcing her to meet his eyes. He quirked an eyebrow in her direction, laughter peeping out from his dark-lashed eyes.

"Can't or won't, my dear Miss Standish?"

Ellie forgot to breathe for a moment...or two. Stars swam before her eyes. Was this what they called starry-eyed?

She inhaled deeply, dragging much needed oxygen into her lungs. No, she couldn't possibly tell him her thoughts.

"Won't, Mr. Chamberlain. Won't." She gently pulled his hand from her chin, resisted a compelling urge to bring the hand to her lips, and leaned her head back to close her eyes and give her overworked, racing heart a much-needed rest.

"We are not done yet, Ellie. You may sleep now, but we are not done, you and I." She knew he leaned close to whisper—close enough to bring goose bumps to her arms and strange stirrings to other body parts—but she kept her eyes firmly shut, though she couldn't prevent a quick grin in response.

The steady thud of the horses' hooves and regular rocking of the carriage lulled her into drowsiness, with the warm, intimate feel of Robert's breath lingering against her ear. Who knew Victorian men could be so...so...sensual? On that thought, Ellie slipped off the precipice...in more ways than one.

Chapter Seven

It seemed like only moments had passed before she felt Robert shaking her.

"Ellie, we're here. Wake up."

Ellie opened her eyes to find her face pressed against Robert's chest, his arm around her shoulders. She gasped and pulled herself from his arms into a stiffly upright position, with a wary glance in Mrs. Chamberlain's direction.

Robert leaned near. "It is all right, Ellie. They are both asleep, but I must wake them now. I...em...enjoyed the short nap."

Ellie shook her head and bopped him lightly on the arm.

"You shouldn't have let me sleep like that. I don't know what your grandmother would have said," she hissed.

Robert grinned unabashedly. "We will never know." The driver came around to open the carriage door. Ellie tried to see over Robert's shoulder but could not. He reached over to touch his sister's arm.

"Melinda, wake up. We're home...at last." Melinda roused with a sleepy smile and turned to wake her grandmother.

Robert stepped down from the carriage and held out a hand to Ellie. She laid her hand in his and climbed down the stairs. As he turned to help the other women, Ellie moved away to stare at the house up on the hill. It was an old Queen Anne-style house, but it was...new. She still couldn't grasp the concept. What she'd previously considered old-fashioned, antique, historical...was now new, modern, state-of-the-art!

Lights spilled out from the three-story house onto the street below. The door stood open and an older man in a dark suit hurried down the steep steps. Ellie's eyebrows shot up and she counted the brick steps as best she could

61

at night—all thirty of them. She turned around to watch Mrs. Chamberlain being handed down from the carriage. How did the woman do it?

The older man bounded down the last step with a puff, threw a curious glance in Ellie's direction, and moved toward Mrs. Chamberlain while Robert handed Melinda down from the carriage.

"Mrs. Chamberlain, Mr. Chamberlain, Miss Melinda. It's so nice to have you home."

"Thank you, Roger. We are exhausted," Robert replied. Roger offered Mrs. Chamberlain a solicitous arm, and turned to head back up the stairs. A sleepy Melinda lifted her skirts to begin what promised to be a long climb and followed her grandmother. Robert turned to offer his arm to Ellie.

"Shall we?"

"Oh, Robert, I'll be hanging onto your arm for dear life by the time we get to the top. You don't want me dragging you down."

Robert laughed. "You say the strangest things, Ellie. Of course I want you *dragging* me down. Why else would I offer you my arm?"

She took it reluctantly, hoping against all odds that she wouldn't embarrass herself by huffing and puffing all the way up the steep stairs.

"Robert, do you walk up these stairs every day? How does your grandmother do it?"

He chuckled. "No, I most certainly do not. Some construction is being done to the back of the house, and the carriage is not able to discharge us there at the moment." He heaved a sigh. "So, for now, we must climb the stairs. I expect work to be completed by the end of next week."

Ellie alternated between watching her step and staring up at the house. The dark sky prevented her from determining its color or features, but the twenty well-lit windows in her immediate view indicated the house was immense.

"Umm...Robert?"

"Yes, Ellie."

"I don't think I asked. What exactly do you do for a living? I suppose I could just as well have ended up in the...umm...immigrant car in my dream."

Robert threw back his head and laughed that wonderfully joyous sound she had come to crave. Melinda turned around and smiled.

"Ellie, Ellie. You make me laugh like I have not in years." He pressed her arm closer to his side.

Ellie had all she could do not to start gasping for air at the effects of his nearness and the steepness of the ascent. She tried to drag in air between her teeth as quietly as possible.

"I am a banker...as was my father before me. This was my parents' house. They left it to me."

"Not to Melinda?"

He gave her a curious look. "No, not to Melinda. She has money in trust, which I manage, but daughters do not usually inherit property."

Ellie studied the back of the young woman ahead of her and shook her head.

"I'd forgotten. How archaic!" she muttered.

"How so, Ellie?"

"I just want you to know that in my time women have as many legal rights as men. So, hang on to your derby, Robert, because the times they are a-changing." She turned a firm, challenging eye on him, to which he responded with a dimpled grin.

"I cannot wait to hear about all the changes, my dear Miss Standish, and I look forward to their challenge as well as to that light in your eyes."

Ellie's face flamed, and she turned her face forward. Mrs. Chamberlain's slow progress halted them halfway up the stairs.

"You really need to get that construction done," Ellie muttered, as an excuse to inhale deeply.

"Yes, I know. I will press the crew tomorrow. This should have been finished while we were gone."

"You said the house had been left to you. Have your parents passed away, Robert?"

He gave her a brief nod. "Yes, they both contracted pneumonia five years ago and died within days of each other, when Melinda was thirteen."

"Oh, Robert, I'm so sorry!"

He laid a warm hand on hers as she clung to his arm.

63

"Thank you. It is one of the diseases that I hope has been eradicated in your time. Has it, Ellie?"

Ellie bit her lip and sighed, though short of breath.

"No, I'm afraid not, Robert. More people survive pneumonia than they used to, but I'm afraid people do still die from it."

"I'm sorry to hear that. And your family, Ellie? What of them? Will they miss you? Did you leave anyone behind?"

Kyle's face flashed before her eyes, and she wondered if she were lightheaded from the climb.

"No, no one, Robert," she lied. "I left no one behind. My parents passed away several years ago in an accident, and I am an only child. Of course, as you know, I think I'm dreaming, so I'm likely to wake up at any time, though I hope not."

They neared the top. Robert pulled her up the last two steps and turned to face her.

"If you *are* dreaming, Ellie, I hope you don't wake up in the near future. If you have traveled back in time, then you have come for a reason, and we must discover what that is. I have my suspicions."

Ellie shook her head and smiled but said nothing. It would be interesting to travel in time, but she'd never heard of anyone who actually had in reality...and she, Ellie, would hardly be the first person to do so. More likely, that would be some physicist or somebody with a government black-ops program.

They followed Mrs. Chamberlain, Melinda and Roger through the front door and into a large, circular foyer crowned by a massive, sparkling chandelier which hung down the length of a round staircase leading to the second and third stories. The chandelier's light shone brightly on the foyer's pale cream paint and reflected off the highly varnished parquet oak floors.

An older woman in a plain, dark gray dress stepped forward.

"Thank you, Mr. White. I'll take Mrs. Chamberlain from here." She took the frail-looking older woman by the arm and began to ascend the stairs.

"Thank you, Mrs. White. I'll see about organizing some tea. Would you care for some refreshment before you retire, Mr. Chamberlain?"

Robert removed his hat and laid it on the magnificent oval teak table in the middle of the foyer. He turned to Melinda with an inquiring look.

"Nothing for me, thank you, Robert, Mr. White. I think I'll just go to bed." She followed the two older women up the stairs.

Robert intercepted the butler's curious stare at Ellie.

"Yes, Roger, I would like some tea. Two cups, please. Could you ask Sarah to prepare a guest bedroom for Miss Standish, please? She will be staying with us for a period of time."

Ellie winced as the butler studied her clothing for a brief moment before responding.

"Certainly, sir. Where will you take your tea?"

"The study, I think, Roger. When you and Sarah are finished, you can retire. I apologize for keeping everyone awake so late tonight. The train schedule is unforgiving."

Roger nodded. "Think nothing of it, Mr. Chamberlain." He moved away, leaving Ellie standing alone in the foyer with Robert.

Ellie dropped her eyes to the floor with the thought that in a romantic movie, alone at last, she and Robert would now be rushing into each other's arms. If this were a dream, why wasn't that occurring? What kind of rip-off dream was this, anyway? She choked on a slightly hysterical giggle.

"Ellie?" Robert's voice penetrated her rambling consciousness.

She looked up to see him gesturing toward a large, closed, paneled door.

"Would you care to join me in the study while your room is being prepared?"

"Oh, sure," she murmured with a barely suppressed chuckle and moved toward the door.

Robert followed and reached from behind to open the door. A shiver ran up her spine as she moved past him. "You're giggling again, Ellie. I suppose you still won't tell me why."

With shaking shoulders, she turned her head from side to side. "I can't, Robert. I'd be too embarrassed."

"Embarrassed? You? Surely not." He gave an

exaggerated sigh and grinned. "Very well. I'll be patient. You will tell me one day."

Ellie entered a massive room done in dark wood paneling. Long green velvet curtains framed highly polished shelves housing hundreds of hardback books. Several elegant brown velvet chairs rested on an immense golden oriental carpet and faced a massive brick fireplace. A large wooden desk occupied one third of the room.

Ellie dropped into one of the chairs indicated by Robert, finding it surprisingly soft and comfortable. She felt instantly at home and wriggled into the chair.

"Oh, Robert, this room is beautiful, absolutely beautiful," she breathed as she stared at the carved teak mantelpiece and eye-catching gilded mirror above it.

Robert lowered himself into the chair opposite hers. He surveyed the room thoughtfully.

"Thank you. I'm glad you like it. The house was built by my father, but I decorated this room last year."

"Well, you did a fine job. It is truly wonderful."

He smiled. "You may use it when you like. Grandmother and Melinda do not like the room. They think it is too dark, and they prefer the parlor."

"Well, thank you. I will."

Robert consulted his pocket watch. "It is past one o'clock in the morning. You must be tired."

Ellie grinned. "I am, though I'm not sure what time it is in *my* time. For all I know, I could be getting plenty of rest right now while I sleep."

He narrowed his eyes and fixed her with an exasperated smile.

"Time," he murmured as he crossed his legs and laced his fingers together.

"Dream," Ellie chuckled teasingly.

Roger entered with a tea tray which he set down on a mahogany table between them.

"Cream and sugar, Miss Standish?"

"No, thanks, Roger." She took her steaming cup and admired the delicate gold leaf embossing small roses on the fine white porcelain.

"Thank you, Roger. I will see you in the morning. Not too early, mind you. I'll leave for the office at ten."

"Good night, sir, Miss Standish." Roger closed the

door quietly behind him.

Ellie again dropped her eyes to her cup.

"You know, Robert, we have huge mugs to drink tea from now...like your shaving mugs. You do have a shaving mug, don't you?"

"Tea from shaving mugs?" He lifted a skeptical eyebrow. "I cannot imagine. Yes, I have a shaving mug. How did you know?"

"I don't know if you remember, but the Victorian era is one of my areas of interest. I have studied it quite a bit, especially women's rights."

He took a sip of tea and eyed her over the rim of the cup. "Ah, yes, women's rights. Melinda...inheritance. Shall I be hearing about that often from you in the future?" A sly grin goaded Ellie.

"You most certainly will, Mr. Chamberlain. If this isn't a dream and I've traveled back in time—as you believe—then that might very well be my reason for being here."

"*That* being what, Miss Standish?" A playful light in his green eyes threatened to make her laugh, but she refused.

"*That* being to educate you and your ilk on the notion that women are equal to men."

"My *ilk*, Miss Standish? My *ilk?*" he murmured with a twitch of his lips.

Ellie pumped her eyebrows comically. "You like that, eh, Mr. Chamberlain? I'm just trying to remember some old-fashioned words and use them...in honor of my visit to your time." She inclined her head graciously in his direction.

Robert sputtered his tea and set the cup and saucer down with a clatter. He leaned forward, rested his elbows on his knees and buried his face in his hands. Ellie watched his shaking shoulders with apprehension.

He dropped his hands to reveal his face convulsed with laughter.

"Oh, my dear Miss Standish! How is my century going to cope with you? How will *I* cope with you?" He shook his head in mock despair.

"As a true Victorian gentleman, Mr. Standish. Unfortunately, as a true Victorian gentleman," Ellie murmured partially under her breath as she longed to throw herself onto his lap and run her fingers through the chestnut waves of his shining hair. Her dream rapidly promised to turn into an epic of unrequited passion and bittersweet yearning.

****

Robert leapt out of bed and rang the bell for his valet. He could not wait to begin the day, to see Ellie once again, to listen to her strange expressions and watch the charmingly rosy color flow and ebb in her face.

With a knock on the door, his long-time valet, Charles, entered the room, an older gentleman who had been in service with Robert's father.

Charles crossed over to open the curtains.

"You are up bright and early, sir."

Robert paced the room like a caged tiger...or a tiger near its mate. He rubbed his hands together briskly.

"Yes, I am, Charles. I could not sleep but merely waited for the sun to come up." Robert crossed to the window and stared out over the city as Charles laid out his clothing. "And the sun has certainly come up. Isn't it a beautiful day?"

He turned from the window to catch Charles' startled look.

"Yes, I know what you are thinking, my good man. What has possessed Mr. Chamberlain, eh?"

Charles pressed his thin lips together and handed Robert his trousers.

"No, sir, I would not presume."

Robert glanced up quickly and grinned.

"Of course you would presume, Charles. You would never tell me, that is all."

"As you like, sir," Charles stoically handed Robert his undershirt.

Robert slipped the soft cotton undershirt on and paused for a moment as if listening. He put a finger to his lips.

"Do you hear anything in the hall, Charles? Is anyone else awake?" Robert crossed to the door and pulled it open, peeking out into the empty hallway. He sighed and closed it quietly.

"We have a guest, you know, Charles. A woman. Her

name is Ellie."

"Yes, sir, I heard," Charles responded as he handed Robert a freshly starched white linen shirt.

"Yes, you probably have. She is from Chicago. She will be a guest with us for a while. For some time, I hope."

"Indeed, sir. How fortunate."

Robert paused and looked over at Charles. "Charles, I know you well. What is it?"

Charles hesitated, then handed his employer a charcoal blue vest.

"Nothing, sir. We heard about Miss Standish's arrival this morning. She sounds like a lovely young woman."

Robert shrugged on his jacket.

"Yes, lovely. Yes, she certainly is lovely. Indeed. I think I will leave work early today and take Miss Standish on a tour of the city. Does that sound like something that might be of interest to a woman, Charles?"

Charles dropped the tie he was handing Robert and bent to pick it up. His face was impassive as he held it out. Robert eyed him with narrowed eyes. How did the man manage to hide all emotion? Robert hoped he had startled the long-time servant, but other than dropping the tie, Charles had betrayed no surprise at Robert's unexpected scheme.

"Certainly, sir. A wonderful idea! So, you will leave work early?"

"Yes, Charles. I will. I will stop by the bank and see if anything pressing requires my attention, and then I will return." Robert drew in a deep breath. It really was a beautiful day!

****

Sunlight peeped through the thick curtains of Ellie's bedroom to tease her eyes open. She stretched like a cat from the tip of her head to the last little toe, every muscle stiff and sore as if she had indeed traveled back in time and aged a hundred years.

She clasped her hands behind her head and studied the room. The mattress had proven surprisingly soft and comfortable. She didn't know what sort of material filled it, and she didn't want to know. Her pillow felt like down and feathers, and her vegetarian soul cringed at the

69

thought. Well-ironed, white linen sheets caressed her skin...all of her skin. Without a change of clothes, she'd slept naked. And she had dreamed of Robert...a dream within a dream. A heated blush spread throughout her body, and she pulled the quilt up to her chin. In the dream, Robert had discarded his true Victorian gentleman persona and...

Ellie banned the thought, heaved a sigh and turned onto her side. Green velvet curtains failed to block tiny streams of light from spilling into the room. The maid had put her in a whimsically circular room with a four-poster bed and what some might have called antique Queen Anne furniture. Ellie had examined the room and its furnishings thoroughly before she hopped into the massive bed last night. The highly polished furniture shone brightly, without nicks and dings, and smelled of freshly-cut wood. A cedar chest at the foot of the bed lent a wonderful scent to the room. The antique furniture was, in fact, new.

With no idea of the time, Ellie reluctantly crawled out of bed and found her clothes. She gingerly pressed them to her nose and grimaced. Her clothes were ripe from traveling. She slid into the skirt and sweater, wishing she had something fresh to wear, though she drew the line at a corseted gown. Perhaps a nice gingham dress, such as she'd seen photos of pioneer women wearing.

Ellie peeked out into the hallway. What time was it? She'd taken off her watch and left it in her purse, which was somewhere on the train. The modern silver train. She slid out the door and stared up and down the length of the darkened hallway. Which way to go?

Trying to retrace last night's exhausted steps following the maid, Sarah, Ellie turned to the left. She shuffled quietly along the oriental runner until she reached the grand staircase. Sounds from downstairs reached her ears—a feminine voice...perhaps Mrs. White, a younger voice...Sarah?

Ellie crept down the stairs while running her hands lovingly along the wooden banister. Ornately framed portraits and landscapes decorated the rounded walls of the staircase. Her apprehension grew as she neared the first floor. What would she find in the light of day?

She came to a stop at the bottom of the stairs and listened for the sounds of activity. The wonderful smell of cooked food made her mouth water, and she followed her nose. She crossed the hall and entered a formal dining room such as she'd seen only in photographs of Victorian homes. White lace curtains diffused and softened the bright light from outside. A long mahogany dining table sported a white linen and lace runner underneath a festive arrangement of flowers in the center. The room was empty.

She moved through the room in the direction of the delicious smell and the sound of voices. To her right she saw another room, a circular room painted a soft buttercup yellow. A large round table presided in the center of the circle, and seated opposite the door was Robert, looking rested and refreshed, reading a newspaper. His wet hair gleamed in the sunlight flooding the room. When he looked up, her heart melted at the sight of his cheerful grin.

"Ellie! You're awake! Good morning. Here, come sit down with me. We'll have breakfast together."

Robert jumped up and pulled out a chair next to his. Ellie hesitated.

"What's wrong?" He cocked his head to the side.

"I...uh...I haven't had a shower, and my clothes are...um...travel stained." She gulped. "Maybe I should just sit on the other side."

Robert grinned, the charming cleft in his chin deepening.

"Nonsense," he murmured. "Come sit here. I cannot imagine that you would ever smell...that is...not be fresh as a daisy," he finished triumphantly though his face took on a bronze tinge.

Ellie chuckled. "Okay. Don't say I didn't warn you." She slid into the chair next to his.

He made a chucking noise as he returned to his seat. "I apologize. I should have instructed Sarah to show you to the washroom in case you wanted to bathe this morning. Mrs. White will see to it after breakfast." He eyed her speculatively. "You do need some clothes, though. As interesting as yours are, they will only bring

71

uninvited attention. You will need to have something in the current fashion...from this time."

Ellie grinned and shook her head. "Robert, you are such a science fiction fan. What am I going to do with you?"

"Well, I don't know, Ellie. Whatever you like, I suppose. I am at your disposal." He pressed his lips together in a failing effort to stifle a grin, and his green eyes danced.

Sarah, a gangly young girl who appeared to be in her late teens, rushed into the room.

"Oh, Miss Standish, I didn't know you were awake. Mrs. White said I was supposed to show you the washroom as soon as you woke, but I didn't know you were up and about." Her panicked brown eyes flickered from Robert to Ellie and back.

"No need to worry, Sarah. Miss Standish will bathe after breakfast. Could you please bring out some tea and breakfast for her?"

Sarah bobbed. "Right away, sir. Right away." She turned to leave.

"Wait, Sarah!" Ellie called to her escaping back. "Please don't bring anything with meat. I-I'm not sure what you have in there for breakfast, but anything without meat will be fine."

Sarah turned back with an open mouth and a wrinkled brow. "Without meat?" she asked incredulously.

Ellie glanced at Robert for help, only to see him watching the exchange with amusement. He remained mute but gave her an encouraging nod.

She turned back to Sarah.

"Yes, you know, potatoes or eggs. I eat eggs...without the yolk, that is. Or toast! Toast would be just fine."

"I don't know, Miss Standish. I'll have to tell Cook. She'll know what to do." With a last nervous glance in Robert's direction, Sarah fled the room.

"Thank you very much for all the help, Robert." Ellie quirked a wry eyebrow in his direction.

"I thought you handled it yourself beautifully, Ellie. How could I have assisted you?" He raised his hands in a mock helpless gesture.

She sniffed and crossed her arms.

"Eggs...without the yolk? What is this about?"

"Cholesterol, you know? I'm watching my cholesterol. My dad had high cholesterol, and it can be a genetically inherited trait."

"Cholesterol? I take it this is derived from fat."

She nodded. "Well, I'm no nutritionist, but yes, most of it comes from fat."

"We will have to discuss your menu with cook. That means no lard?"

Ellie huffed and shook her head. "Animal fat."

"Cheese?" His smile was rapidly turning into a sly smirk.

"You know I eat cheese. I would like to believe that the milk is humanely obtained."

Robert dropped his smile, and his expression turned grave for a moment.

"I do not know if your visit to the turn of the century is going to make you happy. There are many things here that are not necessarily humane...or safe...or healthy."

Ellie blushed. She was as happy as a clam...in his presence.

"I'm quite content, Robert. Thank you."

He laid a warm hand over hers. "I hope you are, Ellie. I fervently hope that you are."

Ellie's eyes flew to his, and she stilled at the intensity in them. She dropped her gaze and pulled her hand from his, afraid she might lose herself in the depths of his eyes and never come back up for air.

"So, you were saying about clothes?"

He leaned back and took a sip of tea. "For today, I think you should borrow some clothing. Would you prefer to borrow from Melinda or from my grandmother? You are all of similar size." The laughter sprang back into his eyes.

Ellie gave him a severe look, but she couldn't repress a chuckle.

"Melinda, please."

"I will ask her before I leave. I must go in to the office this morning. We will see about buying some clothing for you."

"I couldn't, Robert. That's too much trouble...and expense. I'm just a stranger...and one who might be simply passing through, at that. Please don't spend any money on me."

"You are no stranger to me, Ellie. I may have met you only yesterday, but I know you. I do not believe you are simply *passing through*." Though he didn't move, Ellie felt as if he whispered in her ear. A smile lingered on his face, but his eyes grew dark and solemn.

At his words, Ellie turned startled eyes on him, but was distracted by Sarah's return with another cup of tea and a plate of food which she placed in front of Ellie with a slight clatter.

"Here, miss. This is everything Cook had ready for breakfast without meat." She dashed out quickly.

Ellie's eyes widened at the sight of the extensive quantity of food heaped on the delicate china plate. A large mound of fried potatoes, two pancakes, four pieces of toast and an oversized, glazed, cinnamon roll all begged for attention.

Ellie gasped. "I can't possibly eat all this."

Robert gave a hearty laugh. "I see Mrs. Smith is in rare form today." He leaned forward to study her plate. "She never gives me that much."

"Well, here, have some," Ellie murmured although she had already dug into the potatoes. "This is delicious. My compliments to Mrs. Smith," she mumbled on a bite of toast.

"I will be sure to pass those along to her."

Ellie noticed he stared at her mouth, and she lifted her napkin to her face.

"Do I have crumbs on my face?"

"No, I'm just watching you." He leaned forward conspiratorially. "I was just wondering how they eat in the twenty-first century, but I can see that nothing has changed."

Ellie colored, certain that she did indeed have crumbs on her face. She slowed her pace to an occasional nibble.

"I wonder, Robert." She hesitated. Such an awkward question.

"Yes, Ellie?" Robert swallowed the last of his tea and checked his watch.

"Who is Constance Green?" Ellie studiously examined

the piece of toast in her hand. "Are you and she...?"

"Are we what?" His half smile told her he was being deliberately obtuse.

"You know... Are you...uh...dating?"

"Dating?" His dark eyebrows flew up. "Do you mean are we courting?"

Ellie couldn't remember. Didn't they use the word dating in 1901?

She nodded, her toast suddenly one of the most fascinating objects in the room.

"Yes, courting."

"Why do you ask, Ellie?"

She gave him an exasperated look. The gleam in his eyes matched the dimples in his cheeks.

"Just wondering, Robert. Just wondering." Ellie shrugged with indifference and raised knife and fork to attack a helpless pancake.

"Constance is an old family friend. Her husband was a friend of mine from college."

"Oh. So she's married." Relief flooded through her, and she turned to him with a grin.

He shook his head. "No, Constance is a widow. Her husband died several years ago."

Ellie's spirits drooped again, and she leaned back into her chair and stared at the festive centerpiece of colorful Asiatic lilies. She gave him a speculative look from under her lashes.

"Why aren't you married, Robert?"

Robert burst out laughing. Ellie blushed and glared at him. When he caught his breath, he murmured, "Ellie, that's not the sort of question we usually ask in polite society."

"Well, in my world, we don't really ask strangers such things either, but since I'm not sure how long I'll be here, I thought I'd bypass the niceties."

He held up a hand. "Don't remind me, madam. You are just *passing through,* I believe."

"That's right, mister. *Just passing through.* So, why aren't you married?"

He regarded her with amusement for a moment before answering.

"It's hard to say, Ellie. I've never asked anyone to

marry me. I suppose that would be a fine answer."

"Why not?" she drilled. She studied his face over her cup of tea.

He gave her a harried look and ran a finger around the edge of his collar.

"Well, it's difficult to say. I-I...have not found someone...suitable."

Her eyebrows shot up. "Suitable?"

"Em...yes. Suitable."

"Really?" She eyed him with skepticism.

"Yes, really."

"And what does suitable mean?"

His cheeks bronzed and he shook his head with a weak smile. "I am not quite certain, Ellie. The word sounded...suitable."

"So, you're *not* waiting for someone suitable."

"No, most likely not."

"Then what are you waiting for?" What a stubborn man!

He adjusted his tie and consulted his watch once again.

"Why are you asking me this, Ellie?" His eyes begged for mercy, but Ellie could not relent.

"I don't know, Robert. I suppose because you won't really say. Now, I'm curious, and I can't seem to let it go." She chuckled. "It's awful of me, isn't it?"

"Yes," he murmured. "It is. You are merciless." His lips curved in a faint smile. With another check of his watch, he stood up and rested a hand on Ellie's shoulder. She fought the urge to rub her face against his warmth like a kitten.

"I must go. I will be back in a few hours. I hope to take you on a tour of the city this afternoon. Would that be acceptable to you? I will speak to Melinda before I leave about some...er...suitable clothing for you."

"Thank you. That sounds wonderful. The tour and the clothing."

"Good. We'll make an afternoon of it. I look forward to it as well."

Her shoulder felt suddenly chilled when he lifted his hand. Watching him cross the room, Ellie admired his tall, lean form in the dark suit and the way his well-trimmed hair kissed the edge of his collar.

He paused at the door and turned slowly, his cheeks still high with color. His gaze flickered beyond her to the window and then back to her face.

"I suppose I have not married because I have never fallen in love before." With a sheepish smile, he turned and left the room.

Chapter Eight

"What do you think about this?" Melinda held up a dark blue silk skirt. It goes with this little bolero jacket." She tossed them on the bed and dragged another outfit from the wardrobe. "Wait. I think this would suit you nicely!" She held up a rose-colored wool skirt and jacket and draped them against Ellie. "This is the one! Do you like it? Put it on. Let's see if it fits."

Ellie envied Melinda her youthful enthusiasm. Had she herself ever been that bubbly as a young woman? She thought back over her years of study, long hours in the library with her head stuck between the pages of a book while other girls fell in love and went on dates.

"Come on, Ellie. If you are shy, I can turn my back."

"Thanks, Melinda, if you wouldn't mind."

Melinda, not yet dressed for the day but decidedly attractive in a pale peach and white tea gown, drifted away to sit in a lovely blue brocade chair. She turned her head away.

"Wait, what about a blouse? Don't I need a blouse?"

Melinda jumped up. "How silly of me. I forgot. Of course you do." She crossed over to her wardrobe and pulled out a white ruffled creation from a large selection of similar white blouses.

"Here," she said as she handed the white batiste blouse to Ellie and sped back to her chair to turn her head toward the wall once again.

Ellie laid the clothing out on the bed and kept a wary eye on Melinda. She'd hated physical education classes for the very same reason—changing in front of other girls. Melinda kept her head firmly turned away.

"I don't hear anything. Are you changing? You don't want me to get a crick in my neck, do you?"

"I'm hurrying...if I can...figure out...how to get this..."

Ellie pulled her bulky turtleneck sweater up and over her head and dropped her skirt. She rolled her eyes as she surveyed her undergarments. Why couldn't she have been blessed with an overnight bag for her dream...or travel...just a small carryall with an extra pair of underwear, a clean, crisp bra, a toothbrush and some deodorant.

Ellie stepped into the soft rose wool skirt and pulled it up, dismayed at the tight fit over her hips. She suspected she'd have to sit very carefully in order to prevent the seams from ripping. She grabbed the blouse and tussled with the small buttons and extra unidentified material. Ellie tried to remember photos she had seen of the fashions of the time. The extra fabric had to be some sort of bow or tie for the neckline. She slipped into the soft blouse and pushed her arms through the long sleeves which were narrow along the lower arms and wrists but puffed to gigantic proportions at the shoulders and upper arms.

Ellie giggled. She couldn't possibly wear this in public.

"Are you dressed, Ellie?"

She choked back a gurgle of laughter. "Not yet. One more minute." Ellie reached to zip up the skirt but it stuck. No amount of tugging would free it.

"Can you come help me, Melinda? I'm stuck."

Melinda turned and jumped up. She began to laugh, this time without hiding it behind her hand. As frustrated as Ellie was, she responded to the infectious tinkling sound with a grin.

"Oh, Ellie, you look a fright. Let me see." She turned Ellie to face her and surveyed her critically. "Well, you must tie the bow of course. What is wrong with the skirt?" She reached for it and tugged. It did not budge.

"Em...Ellie? It doesn't fit. Are you wearing a corset?" Melinda's cheeks took on a pink tinge.

Ellie's eyebrows shot up. "A corset? Certainly not!"

Melinda nodded sagely and stepped back. "Well, I am afraid the skirt will not fit without a corset. It was designed to be worn with a smaller waist. *I* cannot wear it without a corset. We'd better find one for you."

"No," Ellie squeaked, bringing Melinda to an abrupt halt as she headed for the wardrobe. "I-I can't wear a corset."

Melinda turned slowly, tilted her head and regarded Ellie with wide blue eyes. "Why ever not, Ellie? All proper women wear corsets. Even grandmother."

Ellie wanted to sink into a chair, but the tightness of the skirt prevented it. She bit her tongue against her first instinct to rant about the sexism of squeezing a female form into a binding corset as she studied Melinda's innocent face. It seemed obvious that women perpetuated their own fashion crimes...especially among the upper classes.

"I-I don't think I can squeeze into one."

Melinda's eyes widened. "Are you saying you've never worn a corset, Ellie? How is that possible?"

Ellie bit her lip. "Umm...we just don't wear corsets where I come from, Melinda."

"Really?" Her eyes almost popped.

"Really." Ellie nodded.

"Well, that's just not possible here. You must wear one, certainly if you want to get into any of my clothes. They are all designed to be worn with a corset." She moved toward her wardrobe. "And you want to go out in the carriage and see the city today with Robert, don't you?"

The thought of spending more time in Robert's company clinched the deal. Ellie suspected Melinda might have great success selling used cars.

"All right," she sighed. "Then I think I'm going to need...umm..."

"You'll need a chemise and a corset cover and several petticoats." The fashion crisis averted, Melinda bustled around importantly, pulling white garments from drawers. "I'd better summon my maid, Alice, to help." She handed Ellie the soft white underclothing and crossed the room to pull on a small cord hidden near the curtains.

Ellie stared at the pile of clothing in her hand, uppermost of which was a dauntingly heavy and stiff corset with deceptively soft and feminine pink ribbons.

"How am I going to wear all this underneath, when I can't even squeeze into the skirt as it is?"

Melinda crossed her arms and regarded Ellie with a matronly expression.

"You'll manage. We all manage."

A tap on the door heralded the arrival of a petite maid dressed in the ubiquitous plain gray servant's dress. Ellie eyed her with suspicion. It seemed obvious that the tiny, freckle-faced, redheaded maid had never had to wear a corset in her life.

"Yes, miss?"

"Alice, could you please help Miss Standish into these garments? I am going downstairs to have some tea and breakfast while you dress." She moved toward the door. "Oh, and could you dress her hair? An upsweep. You know what I like, Alice."

Alice bobbed at the closing door and turned to Ellie.

Ellie held up a hand to ward her off. "Wait, Alice. Just a minute. I can get into this...um...chemise by myself. Could you turn around while I just get into it?"

"Yes, miss." Alice's brown eyes popped, but she rotated and faced the wall.

Ellie managed first to extricate herself from the tight clothing and then slipped out of her bra and underwear, promising to give them a good washing in the bathroom sink when she returned to her room.

She sorted through the undergarments and pulled out something that remotely resembled pictures of a chemise. She shook the simple white linen garment out and slipped it over her head. Conscious of a draft on her nether regions, she grabbed a pair of drawers and slipped them on...knowing she would never be able to return these intimate garments to Melinda. But one look at the clothing spilling from Melinda's wardrobe suggested she would hardly miss a few things.

With still more white lacy undergarments in her hand, Ellie drew a blank.

"Okay, Alice, I'm lost. What is this thing?"

Alice turned and blinked. She moved forward hesitantly.

"Why, it's a corset cover, miss. It goes over the corset."

"So, what do I put on next?"

"The corset, miss. I can help you with that."

If Alice had questions, as her wide-eyed look suggested, she was too polite to ask.

"If you would raise your arms, miss."

81

Alice took the beribboned corset and wrapped it around Ellie's waist. Ellie instinctively sucked her stomach in and straightened.

"I'm just going to tighten it now," Alice murmured.

As Ellie felt the corset begin to mold to her body, she noticed her upper torso pushed forward while her rear bent backward. Something was seriously wrong. She couldn't breathe.

"Wait, Alice, wait." Ellie took a shallow breath and murmured. "Is this thing on straight? I'm practically bent over."

"Yes, miss, that's the way it's supposed to look. It's an S-bend corset. All the ladies wear them."

Ellie twisted her neck to quirk an eyebrow at Alice.

"I don't think you have one on, do you, Alice?"

Alice's face turned pink. "Me? Oh no, miss. The servants don't wear them." She began to pull again. "Actually, I think only the wealthy ladies wear them."

"You must be kidding. Why, for Pete's sake?"

"Why...to look beautiful, ma'am. With small waists and rounded... Well, you know what I mean. I wish I could wear one. They're so pretty."

Ellie grunted. "I can't breathe. Can you loosen it?"

"No, miss. This is as loose as I can make it. You will get used to it. Miss Melinda used to cry when she first started wearing hers, but she doesn't any more. Are you ready for the petticoats?"

"I feel like a pigeon. My chest is sticking out." Ellie tried desperately to straighten but the corset kept her bent. "Petticoats? There's more than one?"

"Yes, miss."

Alice helped her step into not one but two white linen petticoats adorned with lace and light blue ribbons. Ellie thought it a shame no one would ever see the beautiful undergarments.

Finally, Alice helped her into the original rose-colored tailored skirt, which now magically zipped up all the way. Alice grabbed the blouse and slipped it over Ellie's shoulders. She buttoned the blouse, tucked it inside the waistband of the skirt and tied a decorative bow at the neck.

"Should we do your hair before we put the jacket on?

Do you have shoes?"

Unable to bend her ribcage to see her feet, Ellie stuck out a bare toe.

"Oh, dear, miss. You need shoes, stockings and garters. Let me see if Miss Melinda has anything. You may have the same size feet." Alice moved away to the magic cupboard and pulled out a pair of silk stockings and a set of little black boots.

"You'd better have a seat here, and I'll put these on. I'm sorry, miss. I should have helped you put these on earlier. We're going about this backward." She busied herself pulling up the stockings and sliding garter belts up to Ellie's thighs.

Ellie's face flamed at the intimacy. "That's all right, Alice. It was my fault. I put on the undergarments out of sequence, I think."

Alice tied the boots and stood back. Ellie held out a helpless hand. Alice grinned and pulled her up.

"There, now. You look lovely, ma'am. How do you feel?" She pulled Ellie toward a white-painted dressing table crowned by a charming oval mirror. Ellie sank onto the small blue velvet stool, doing her best to sit as straight as an S-bend corset would allow.

"I'm miserable, Alice, but thank you for all your hard work."

"It will get easier, miss," she murmured. "Don't you worry. Women dress this way every day." She undid Ellie's braid and began to brush her long hair with a silver-backed brush in long, soothing strokes. Ellie had a quick recollection of her mother brushing her hair in just that way before bedtime.

A knock on the door brought Melinda back into the room. Ellie looked at her in the mirror, gaining a new respect for the uncorseted tea gown she wore.

"You look beautiful, Ellie, just beautiful." She flitted across the room and pulled a small, rose velvet chair next to Ellie. "How do you feel?"

Ellie gave her a wry smile. "As I mentioned to Alice here...miserable. I can't believe you wear all these clothes every day."

Melinda sighed. "I know." She brightened. "Still, it certainly displays your tiny waist to perfection."

83

Ellie tried to glance down at her so-called "tiny waist," but Alice had a mass of hair in her hand which prevented any movement.

"Mmmmm, thank you."

"So, tell me about Chicago, Ellie. That's where you come from, isn't it? How is it they don't wear corsets in Chicago? I thought it a truly modern city...much like Seattle."

Ellie tried to regress a hundred years.

"Oh, I'm sure they do, Melinda. I-I don't wear them, but I think many women do."

"Hmmm...only the working class does not have to wear..." In the mirror, Ellie saw Melinda bite her lip and blush. "Well, never mind. I know so little about you. Are you married? Do you have family? Where are they? Do they miss you?"

Ellie concentrated on remembering the sequence of questions in the bubbly barrage.

"Wait, let me see. No, I don't have family, my parents passed away several years ago. I'm not married yet, and I doubt if my fiancé misses me—" Ellie froze, her heart in her throat. Maybe Melinda missed it. She didn't.

"Your fiancé? Are you to be married then?" Melinda's blue eyes popped and she clapped her hands. "How exciting! What is his name? When?"

Ellie swallowed hard and wondered if she could ask for Melinda's confidence. To what end? Melinda would only wonder why Ellie wanted to hide her engagement.

"Oh, Melinda, I shouldn't have mentioned that. It's not a big thing...really. I don't know when." She sniffed. "Maybe never. Forget I ever said anything."

Melinda stuck out a pink lower lip and eyed Ellie with concern.

"Not a big thing," she repeated in the tone of someone savoring an unfamiliar expression. She nodded. "I take it you do not wish to discuss it, then. I understand. It is a private matter. I apologize for prying." Melinda jumped up in a restless movement. "Still though, I would love to be engaged." She twirled around the room with her arms wide. "Parties and balls and dinners and breakfasts...plus a handsome man at my side. Wouldn't it be wonderful?"

Ellie watched her with a stirring of affection. An

engagement would come soon if Melinda had anything to say about it. Alice was working miracles into what Ellie recognized as a Gibson hairdo—a glorious upswept style guaranteed to make any woman look tall and elegant.

"So, you want to be married."

Melinda stopped dancing and plopped down on the chair once again with a whiff of lavender. "I do not know that I want to be married yet, but I would love to be engaged. That would be exciting. Some of my friends want to marry so they can be free to set up their own homes, but Robert lets me do as I please, and I do not feel restricted here. I would like to be in love." Her voice trailed away on a sigh.

Ellie couldn't help herself and matched Melinda's contagious sigh, the memory of a pair of green eyes tugging at her heart. "I know what you mean."

Melinda's sharp ears turned toward Ellie. "But you are already engaged." She bit her lower lip. "Sorry, I apologize. I am such a busybody." She jumped up and glided toward her wardrobe. "Hurry, Alice. I have to dress for Amy's tea party this afternoon."

"Yes, miss."

"I didn't know you were going out. So, you're not coming on the tour, then?"

"Oh no, that is just you and Robert. Grandmother feels unwell, and I have the party to attend."

"Oh."

Melinda misunderstood. "You will have an enjoyable time. Robert is a wonderful man, kind and gentle. There is no need to be afraid of him."

"I don't doubt it." Alice stuck a sprig of small silk roses and baby's breath into the crown of Ellie's hair. Freed from the maid's ministrations, Ellie turned to watch Melinda. She chewed on her lip for a moment and drew in a deep breath.

"Melinda, why hasn't Robert married before now?"

Melinda rummaged through her undergarment drawers, tossing aside one petticoat after another.

"What?" she asked distractedly. "Robert? I do not know why he has not found a wife, really. I tease him about being a confirmed bachelor all the time. He is in his late 30s, you know. Quite old." She grinned and continued

85

ransacking her wardrobe.

Ellie held out her hand to Alice with beseeching eyes. Alice grinned and pulled her upright. She almost toppled over and leaned on Alice while she regained her balance.

Melinda continued. "Although that may change soon. Constance has her eye on him, you know."

"I didn't know," Ellie murmured with a pain in her chest. The corset...too tight.

"Yes. She has not said anything to me directly, but I have seen the way she looks at Robert...ever since her husband died."

"Really..."

"Grandmother thinks she is too old for Robert. She says that Robert needs to look for a young woman who can give him children. I think Constance is the same age as Robert."

Ellie felt faint. Her thirty-fifth birthday had come and gone.

"But Constance can still have children in her thirties." Ellie knew she defended herself.

"Yes, but Grandmother still thinks she is too old for Robert. She wants Robert to marry someone in her early twenties."

Melinda finally found a few garments that pleased her and tossed them on the bed.

"Are you feeling well, Ellie? You look positively green. Is the corset too tight?" Melinda moved toward her and raised a motherly hand to Ellie's forehead.

"I'm fine. It is tight, but Alice says it's as loose as it can be. I'll be fine."

"Well, you look absolutely stunning."

Ellie shrugged on the matching rose bolero jacket and surveyed herself in the mirror. Her face did look pale, but she had to admit she looked very...Victorian. Her ash-brown hair shone from Alice's brushing, and the upswept style suited Ellie's oval face. The clothing, although miserably uncomfortable, gave her an elegant height she'd never known in all her vertically-challenged years. She preened.

"Thank you. I do look quite regal, if I may say so."

Melinda laughed and turned away. "I must get dressed myself. Robert should be here soon. I will see you this evening at dinner."

Ellie's best intentions to sashay to the door were hampered by the corset and the boots which covered her feet somewhere far below her skirts. She managed a stilted prance until she got through the door.

She leaned on the wall to catch her breath and eyed the round staircase which once seemed so charming but now loomed terrifyingly as a death-defying stunt. The bedroom door flew open, and Melinda erupted into the hallway.

"Wait, Ellie. You forgot your hat. No well-bred lady goes outside without a hat."

"A hat? On this fabulous hairdo?"

Melinda laughed and dragged her back inside. From the nether regions of the mysterious wardrobe, Alice brought out a large, black, velvet hat trimmed with rose-colored ribbons.

"Sit down, Ellie. Alice cannot put it on your head if you do not sit down."

Ellie eyed the stool, remembering she had to be levered off it. She sighed.

Alice perched the dark hat atop Ellie's hairdo at an angle which dipped toward her right eye. Ellie rolled her eyes. She couldn't see anything but the brim of the hat above her nose. In the mirror, she saw Alice approach with a long pearl-tipped hatpin that she stuck into the hat and through the bun on top of her hair.

Melinda hovered.

"There now. You look ravishing. Off you go."

Ellie put a tentative hand to the creation on her head to see if it would move with her...or against her. It stayed in place. She twisted her neck gingerly to eye Alice, who grinned and pulled her upright.

Once outside the door, Ellie again paused to lean a hand against the wall. As if matters had not already been treacherous with the unfamiliar boots, the corset, her bizarre posture and the heavy hairdo, now she needed to contend with a heavy, oversized, albeit beautiful, hat which threatened to throw her off balance.

She moved to the head of the stairs and gripped the railing. Tilting her head back as best she could to counterbalance her weight, she stepped down gingerly, feeling her way down the stairs one step at a time since she could not look down to see her feet. Halfway down the interminable descent, the front door of the foyer opened and Robert came into view. He looked up, and his eyes widened. Ellie heard his quick intake of breath. She paused for a moment and gulped, hoping she wouldn't disgrace herself with a tumble down the stairs. His lips curved into a slow smile, and Ellie's knees wobbled in response.

"Ellie, you look absolutely beautiful." He moved to take the steps two at a time arriving to hold out his arm. "May I?"

Ellie nodded mutely, and she gratefully took his arm. Once they reached the bottom step, Robert stood back and surveyed her once again. Ellie's face burned, and she attempted to take a deep breath.

"I knew you were beautiful, Ellie, but I had no idea how charming you would look in *my time*." He grinned.

"Thank you, Robert, but I have to tell you *your time* is killing me." She grimaced. "There is absolutely no question of my eating or drinking while I am in this costume."

His eyes ran up and down her body rakishly. "Yes, I can see that you are much more...em...restricted than you were in your other clothing."

She laid a hand on the table for support.

"I'll say."

"Shall we?" He took her arm and led her outside. Ellie paused on the elegant wraparound porch and stared at the city below. No skyscrapers towered above this turn-of-the-century city of rolling greenery and sparkling blue lakes. A light haze of pollution hung in the moist air, settling over the panoramic vista. From the landmarks, she recognized their location. The Chamberlains lived on Queen Anne Hill, so named for the number of homes built at the end of the nineteenth century in the Queen Anne style of architecture.

"What are you thinking?" Robert murmured as they descended the stairs.

"Oh, gosh, lots of things! How different the city looks, how much pollution already hangs in the air, yet how beautiful it still is."

"It is a beautiful city, isn't it? You will have to tell me about this...em...pollution some time. I would be interested to hear of that."

Despite Ellie's unfamiliarity with the mechanics of her voluminous clothing and her inability to see her feet, their descent of the stairs was quicker today than the ascent the night before, and Robert handed Ellie up into the carriage. She put out a protective hand to guard her hat while trying to hoist her skirts up with the other, and she wondered how women got anything done in this century, hampered as they were by their clothing. She remembered, though, that while upper-class women were restricted in their movements and could do little significant manual labor, they did contribute heavily with time and energy to charitable works.

Robert climbed in beside her, and the carriage moved off. Ellie sat awkwardly forward not only because the bend of the corset required it but because the wide brim of her hat needed extra room. She tried to turn toward Robert but hit him in the face accidentally.

"Oops, sorry. I'm trying to get used to this thing."

He laughed. "I'm sure you are. Women have taken to wearing larger and larger hats recently. I suspect it has very little to do with keeping their heads warm and more to do with outshining each other."

"You're probably right, Robert. And believe me, that will not change by the twenty-first century."

He laughed with his endearingly unique male resonance and touched her hand briefly. Ellie had enough trouble gasping for air in her corset without having her breath stolen by his charm.

Robert proved to be a wonderfully insightful tour guide. Giving in to her requests to see specific sites, he took her down to a vendor's market, the forerunner of the modern Pike's Place Market, she realized. As they wandered the covered stalls, she described how it would look...as well as she could remember, having only been to the market once before. She asked to go down to the waterfront, but he vetoed that as being too rough a neighborhood for a lady.

"It's quite trendy now, you know, with restaurants and musicians and lots and lots of tourists," she murmured with a sigh.

"Trendy? What does that mean?"

Ellie loved stumping this normally confident man with strange terms. The confusion on his face gave him such a vulnerable look.

"Popular."

"Ah...popular." He nodded. "Trendy," he repeated to himself.

"I wanted to get a closer look at the clipper ships in the bay. We don't have those anymore...or if we do, they're very rare...historic."

"You can see the ships in the bay from any window in the front of the house. They are much more attractive from a distance."

"Really?" She sighed.

He gave her a sympathetic look. "Would you like to have some lunch at a park? I had Mrs. Smith put a picnic together for us."

She turned to him with a pleased smile. "Why Robert, that would be wonderful! Yes, let's go to the park."

A half hour later, the driver pulled into a lovely park on a beautiful blue lake. Robert helped Ellie down while the driver unloaded several baskets from the coach. After spending the last several hours clutching at her skirts to keep them from the dirt roads of the turn of the century, Ellie was pleased to see a wooden promenade skirting the lake. Small boats took passengers out onto the calm water to lull the day away in the rare sunshine of the often rainy Pacific Northwest.

Ellie hesitated, unsure of what to do, but Robert took her hand in his arm.

"Shall we walk for a while?"

Ellie watched the couples and families strolling along the lake's edge, and she hesitated.

"I don't know, Robert. Teeter-tottering around in this outfit in the vendor's market was one thing. It was too crowded for anyone to notice anything, but these people are strolling. I mean, they're *really* promenading."

Robert laughed, and she tilted her head back at an angle to glare.

"Ellie, I find you extremely amusing. Promenading, indeed. Well, of course, they are. It *is* a promenade."

He turned to the driver, a silent young man with dark hair and a mustache.

"Jimmy, lay our things out over there, please." He nodded in the direction of a picnic area dotted with several black wrought iron tables and chairs. "We will return shortly."

He looked down at her and gave her hand a firm squeeze.

"Shall we, madam?"

He didn't wait for an answer but moved out, his pace slow to accommodate Ellie's unsure steps. Ellie kept her eyes on the boardwalk...for several reasons...one was to watch her footing.

"Ellie, my dear, lift your head. No one will notice anything unusual about you except that you are a beautiful woman." He peered around the corner of her hat. "Although quite fetching, that hat is extremely inconvenient. I cannot see your face."

She tilted her head and turned toward him, knowing her cheeks must be as rosy as her dress.

"There you are," he murmured softly with a dancing light in his eyes.

"Mr. Chamberlain, I believe you are flirting with me." She used her hat to shield her embarrassed face. The large, black, rose-ribboned concoction actually had some value after all.

He paused for a moment, standing stock still so that she had to rotate, since he still held her arm. She ended up facing him. He dipped his head and looked into her eyes with a playful grin.

"Why, Miss Standish, I do believe I am." He reached up with his free hand and softly touched the line of her cheek. Ellie's blush deepened. She longed to rub against his hand but resisted once again.

"Robert. Miss Standish."

Ellie turned quickly, almost knocking herself off balance.

Constance stood in front of them on the promenade, an odd expression on her face. She was accompanied by a younger blonde woman dressed like Constance in a dark blue, tailor-made silk skirt with a white blouse.

Chapter Nine

"Constance. How are you today? I did not expect to see you up and about so early after our late arrival." Robert dipped his hat in her direction.

Ellie nodded a greeting, but ran a quick hand up to steady her hat. She did not miss Constance's frank, appraising stare.

"I promised my niece, Amanda, that I would bring her to the park today. Amanda, you remember Mr. Chamberlain. And this is Miss Standish."

Ellie greeted the young girl, who watched her aunt with adoration.

"Miss Standish, you look quite...stunning today." Constance's voice held some reserve.

Ellie ducked her head. "Thank you, Constance. You also look very...beautiful."

Constance had the grace to blush. She put a hand to her large, dark blue, netted hat.

"Well, thank you. I could murmur *this old thing*, but in fact, it is new."

"Are we still expecting you for supper tonight, Constance?"

Ellie flinched for just a moment, and Robert tightened his arm.

"Yes, Robert, I am still planning to come. Seven p.m., correct?"

Robert nodded with a practiced smile. "Yes, seven it is." He tipped his hat to her. "Well, if you will excuse us, Constance, we must move on. I am doing a poor job of showing Ellie the city."

"Are you new to Seattle then, Miss Standish?" Constance fixed Ellie with dark eyes, an almost imperceptible narrowing the only sign of strong emotion.

Ellie blinked. "Please call me Ellie. Yes, I am new. I've never been here before."

"Well, you have a fine tour guide in Robert."

Constance relaxed her face and nodded. "Please excuse us. I will see you this evening, Robert." She moved away with Amanda, and Ellie resisted the urge to turn around and watch her graceful gait. She was fairly sure she could learn a lot from Constance about the art of feminine elegance in this era.

She moved on with Robert, wincing as they passed an occasional fellow stroller who nodded, tipped his hat or dipped her head and murmured "Good day, Mr. Chamberlain."

"Robert, I didn't realize we would see so many people who know you. What will they think?"

He greeted another couple who nodded at him. "About what, Ellie?"

"About me, I guess. I really feel like I'm sticking out... like they can tell."

"Tell what?" He paused and turned to her. "What can they tell?"

"Well, that I'm..." She ducked her head, but he raised her chin with a gentle index finger, forcing her to meet his green-eyed gaze.

"You're...?"

"Different, odd, out of place," she muttered.

"That's what I love about you, Ellie. You *are* different...from any woman I've ever met." He tapped the tip of her nose and resumed walking.

She trod on in a daze. Had he just said *love*? As *in love*?

"Come, I am famished. Shall we have our luncheon now?" He led the way over to the picnic Jimmy had set up. A large, white, linen tablecloth covered the small, round, wrought iron table. Robert pulled out a matching, black-painted, wrought iron chair and lowered her into it. Jimmy had set out several simple white porcelain plates and plain silverware along with linen napkins.

"Let's see what Cook has prepared for us."

He brought out a plate of roasted chicken, a bowl of potato salad, a packet of cheese, bread, several slices of chocolate cake, bananas, two apples, raisins and almonds. Ellie eyed the large hamper with amazement. It seemed bottomless, like some magician's hat. The food just kept coming.

"Is there anything here that you can eat? I see that there are some things without meat, but will it be enough to satisfy your hunger?"

"I doubt if I can eat anything while I'm wearing this corset, but yes, there is plenty of food." She ran a hand along her narrow waist.

Robert paused and stared at her waist with a frown.

"You must do away with that silly thing. I don't know why women wear them anyway."

Ellie raised an amused eyebrow. "Well, in my case, I can't get into Melinda's clothes without them."

"We should have a seamstress come by tomorrow. She can adjust a few things. Please do not wear that thing again. I do not like to see you so miserable. I want you to be happy here."

"I don't think I'll be able to wear it again. I'm fairly sure I've cracked a rib...or two." She grinned, wondering about the improbability of discussing her underwear with a man she'd met only the day before...in the late Victorian/early Edwardian era.

"Ummm...Robert? Don't you think it's strange that we are discussing my...uh...underwear?"

He ladled some potato salad onto her plate and flashed his dimples. A bronze tinge touched his cheeks.

"Actually, yes, I do, Ellie. Very odd! In fact, I cannot say that I have ever had a discussion with a woman about her...em...undergarments."

Ellie saw an opening and went for it with an arched eyebrow in his direction. "Not once, Robert?"

While Robert busily searched the basket for wine and glasses, Ellie watched with glee as his hands stilled. He turned to her with a decidedly bright red face.

"Em...er...I...em...well...that is..." He scanned a mysterious spot over her shoulder in the distance.

"Oh, Robert, you should see your face." Ellie broke out into a rib-clutching laugh, the more so because her clothes did not allow for expansion. "It's priceless. No need to answer, Mr. Chamberlain. I would assume at your age that you are no...uh...saint."

"Ellie," he reprimanded, his color still high. "I hardly think this is an appropriate...subject for discussion." He tossed back the entire goblet of wine he'd just poured.

She patted his hand, loving him all the more for his vulnerability. "Don't worry, Robert. I won't bring it up again...unless you do."

His color receded, and he reached for a slice of bread with an unsteady hand.

"Thank you," he murmured, busily making a sandwich as if it were the most challenging task he had faced to date.

The imp on Ellie's shoulder goaded her.

"I can wait until you're ready to tell me...whether you've been a saint or not, that is."

She gurgled with laughter when he dropped his sandwich.

"Ellie, I really must insist you stop...em...this line of questioning. It is not seemly."

"I know," she said with a quirked brow and a mischievous grin as she bit into an apple. Undaunted, she continued to chuckle. "I'm from the twenty-first century, you know, Robert. Things are different now."

"Now or then?" he muttered while he tried to pick up the pieces of his bedraggled sandwich.

"Then."

"I see. Well, I'm sure it must be very... ahhh...adventurous in your time, Ellie. We are not so...bold at this time."

"*We* are. Besides, I thought you said you *loved* that about me...that I'm so different. Remember? Just a few moments ago?"

He tossed back another glass of wine and eyed her with a raised brow. "Really, was it only a few moments ago?"

She nodded, forgetting the weight of her hat. "Mmmm-hmmm."

"Very right, then! What about you, Ellie?"

Busily adjusting her hat, which seemed in danger of sliding off her head and taking her hair with it, Ellie lost track of the thread of the conversation.

"What about me?"

Robert rested his arms on the table and leaned forward. "Are you a...a saint?"

As his words sunk in, she stopped fidgeting and stared at him. Color flooded her face. She had never expected proper Robert to tease her back along the same lines. His eyes glittered, and his smile sported a rakish tilt to the corner.

She thought fast and hard. The wrong answer might turn this turn-of-the-century man from her.

"In your time? No, I wouldn't be considered a saint. But in my time? I might as well be."

Nonplussed, he sat back against his chair and toyed with his empty glass.

"What does that mean?"

Ellie grinned. "Maybe I'll tell you someday, Mr. Chamberlain. This food is wonderful." She bit into her food with apparent gusto and said no more. She felt Robert's intent gaze but kept her eyes on the plate in front of her until she saw out of the corner of her eye that he picked up his own food and began to eat.

****

Robert returned to his room from the washroom and sat down to allow Charles to comb his hair and trim the ends.

"How was your outing today, sir?"

Robert looked at the older man in the mirror. He caught sight of his own reflection. For pity's sake, his cheeks were as pink as a girl's. He ran a quick hand along his jaw with a rueful smile and cleared his throat.

"Wonderful, Charles. I had a very pleasant time."

"I am glad to hear it, Mr. Chamberlain. You certainly deserve to take some time from work."

"Yes, it was really very pleasant to walk about during the middle of the day. I don't do it enough. As you see, my face took some sun today."

The comb in Charles' hand stilled for a moment. Robert narrowed his eyes, grinned and dared the older man to say something.

"Yes, sir, of course."

"Oh, Charles, you know I am teasing. Behold me blushing like a child."

"Blushing, sir? I would not have known it was a blush."

Robert jumped up and pulled his dark blue velvet bathrobe closely about him.

"Yes, I had a wonderful time. Pick out some clothing

that suits me well, Charles. I want to look very handsome this evening."

"Mr. Chamberlain, you always look handsome."

Robert's face reddened once again. "Good gravy, it seems even you can make me blush. Have I no self-control?"

"As much as you need, sir. I am certain of that."

With a sigh, Robert shrugged out of his robe and slipped on his undergarments.

"I hope you are right, Charles. I am not as certain of that as you."

He continued to dress in silence as he contemplated the night ahead. Would Ellie dance with him? Would he do her justice or fall all over her feet in an effort to impress her? She had looked quite stunning today in her lovely rose suit, albeit a bit uncomfortable. What would she look like tonight? What did her hair look like down around her shoulders? He longed to find out, but it seemed unlikely that would happen tonight.

****

At 6:30 p.m. Melinda and Alice were still trying to stuff Ellie into an evening dress of dark blue silk.

"Ellie, you really must put the corset on."

"No, please don't make me wear that thing again. My ribs are bruised. Robert said I didn't have to."

Melinda froze. "Robert?" She peered into Ellie's face. "What does he have to do with this? Do not tell me you discussed your...undergarments with him!"

Ellie colored and grinned sheepishly. "Yes?"

"Ellie, you are such a strange creature. Sometimes, it is as if you are from another world. We do not discuss those matters with men, and it is really none of their business."

"Well, then why do we wear these things? If men don't care, why do I have to torture myself in a corset?"

She grimaced and tugged some more. "I have no earthly idea. Alice, why do we wear those silly things?"

Alice's eyes bulged. "Oh, miss, I wouldn't know." She giggled. "I don't even own one."

"Lucky you," Ellie whispered under her breath as she sucked in her stomach to see the dress finally snap into place around her curves. She tested it gingerly by walking across the room. The silk material rustled delightfully, and she felt like a princess going to a ball. Alice had redone her hair to leave a few curls falling to her shoulders. A sprig of glass crystals peeked out from the crown of her hair.

Melinda followed Ellie to the mirror and made some minor adjustments to the off-shoulder gown with its heart-shaped bodice. She stood next to Ellie and surveyed her own golden taffeta dress, similar in style but uniquely flattering to her particular blonde coloring.

"We look very stylish tonight, I must say."

"Yes, we do, don't we?" Ellie murmured. "Is your grandmother coming down to dinner?"

"Yes. We are having quite a few guests tonight, as a matter of fact."

Ellie turned to stare, open-mouthed. "What? Like a dinner party? I thought this was just your family and Constance."

"Oh, no. We have had this planned for some time. I am surprised Robert did not explain. There is to be some dancing afterward."

"Dancing?" Ellie choked. She held up a hand as if to ward off an invisible terror. "Melinda, *I* don't know how to dance. I'll just head to bed early. No wonder Robert didn't mention this. He knew I would take off," she muttered.

"What do you mean *take off?*" Melinda leaned into the mirror and smoothed back a wisp of hair.

"Leave...depart."

Melinda turned to Ellie with a waggling finger. "Well, you are not *taking off* then. You are staying for the evening. We should have great fun. Some of my friends are coming, and there is one young man...James." She blushed. "It will be great fun."

Ellie eyed her skeptically. She tried to smile, but one or both sides of her lips failed to cooperate beyond a slight grimace.

"Are you ready? We should go downstairs."

"As ready as I'll ever be." Ellie tried to take a deep breath but failed. The air seemed thin. "Good night, Alice. Thank you for everything."

"Oh, good night, miss. I've laid out a nightgown for this evening, and a tea gown for the morning."

"Thank you, and thank you so much, Melinda, for loaning me your clothes."

"You are welcome, Ellie. I am happy to see you wear them. I have grown too tall for them."

Ellie hovered in Melinda's shadow as they descended the stairs. She followed Melinda as the younger woman lifted her chin and sailed into the drawing room, where some guests already waited. Ellie found an inconspicuous spot by the wall while she watched Melinda, the first of the family to arrive, work the crowd by welcoming the guests, cooing over beautiful gowns and shaking men's hands. Already quite the accomplished hostess at her young age, she appeared to be in her element.

"You look as bashful as I feel, madam." Ellie jumped when a warm, masculine voice spoke near her ear. She turned to find an attractive blonde, mustached man of medium height smiling at her. He executed a small bow. "How do you do? My name is Stephen Sadler."

"Ellie Standish," she murmured.

"It is a pleasure to meet you, Miss Standish." He nodded toward the group with a small sigh. "I do not know how I manage to allow my sister to bring me to these gatherings. I am usually uncomfortable in large crowds." He nodded his head in the direction of one of Melinda's friends, a young blonde woman in a pale blue gown.

Ellie turned to him with relief. "Me, too. I'm only here because I'm staying with the family."

Stephen regarded her with sympathetic blue eyes and a pleasant smile.

"I see. And will you be visiting for a while?"

Ellie scanned the room briefly and shook her head.

"I don't know. I really don't know."

"Are you new to Seattle, Miss Standish?"

"Please call me Ellie." She turned back to him. A handsome man who appeared to be in his early thirties, Stephen wore a dark blue suit with a pale yellow waistcoat over a well-starched white shirt. "Yes, I am new." Ellie paused. Had she told someone else she was new to Seattle...or that she wasn't? She had to remember to keep the lies straight.

Unsure of what to talk about, she settled for

watching Melinda work her way toward a tall, handsome young man with curly brown hair, who had eyes only for the vision in gold. He blushed when Melinda drew near, and Ellie noticed that Melinda's cheeks took on a rosy hue, as well.

"And where are you visiting from, Ellie?"

"Chicago," she murmured without thinking.

"Chicago! I know it well. My grandfather lives there. I visit there often. Perhaps I have met your family?"

Ellie turned back toward Stephen. "Uh...no, I don't think so. I'm an orphan."

"Oh, dear. I *am* sorry to hear that."

Unexpected tears sprang to her eyes...either at the sincere note in his voice or the fact she'd used the word *orphan* to describe herself. Or maybe she was just homesick and wanted the comfort of her own bed and her own clothes. She'd never had a dream go on this long or continue in such a sequential, story-like fashion.

"Ellie? Miss Standish? Forgive me. Did I say something wrong?" Stephen bent his neck to peer into her eyes. He took one of her hands in a gentle grasp and shook his head. "I can be very tactless. I'm sorry."

She dashed at her eyes and swallowed hard. "Oh, no, you didn't say anything wrong. I don't know what that was. Silly me." She gave him a watery smile.

"I do apologize." He continued to hold her hand and study her face with his soft, sky-blue eyes.

"Please don't worry, Stephen. Whatever that temporary aberration was, it wasn't your fault."

"Sadler. Perhaps you should let my guest have her hand back. You have held onto it long enough."

Chapter Ten

A tight-lipped Robert stood in front of them in a deceptively relaxed posture, his hands behind his back, but Ellie felt the tension in his body even at a distance of three feet.

Stephen looked at Robert for a moment, then to Ellie. He smiled at her and unhurriedly patted her hand before letting it go.

"Robert, how nice to see you." Stephen gazed passively at the taut man in front of him.

"Stephen," Robert nodded briefly. "Miss Standish, I believe it is just about time to go in to supper. Are you ready?"

Ellie looked from Robert to Stephen and back again. The situation felt surreal. They weren't...surely they weren't...staring daggers at each other? Stephen's soft blue eyes grew hard. Robert eyed him narrowly.

"Okay, sure, let's eat." Ellie decided it was time for some good old-fashioned twenty-first-century lingo.

She caught Stephen's startled look as she moved away on Robert's arm.

"What was that about, mister?" she muttered between clenched teeth and a tight smile.

"I would like to know the same thing, madam. Tears in your eyes and some chivalrous hand-holding? If something troubles you, perhaps I may be of assistance." Robert nodded his head graciously at the guests as they started to file out of the room in Melinda's wake. Mrs. Chamberlain walked on the arm of a tall silver-haired gentleman who bent his head to hear the older woman.

"It was nothing. But your behavior was embarrassing. For Pete's sake, the man was just holding my hand," she hissed.

"Yes, madam, I noticed. If I did not know better, I would think you must have known Mr. Sadler for some time." His whisper seemed loud to Ellie's ears.

"What is that supposed to mean? And lower your voice, please. People can hear you."

"It means exactly the way it sounds. Crying on a man's shoulder and holding hands is usually reserved for someone you have known for months...someone who is courting you...at least in *this* century." He cleared his throat. They moved through the foyer and toward the back of the hall into the fabulous dining room, now glistening with sparkling china, crystal stemware and elegant silverware. Harvest gold velvet curtains were drawn against the night, and candles cast a warm, festive glow over the table.

"Don't be such a fuddy-duddy, Robert." She pulled her hand out of his arm, leaving him to lead the way to her seat. He waved away a staff member and pulled out her seat, bending low near her ear to whisper.

"What on earth is a fuddy-duddy, woman?"

"You are!" she flung over her shoulder. She turned away and plastered a pleasant smile on her face. Robert moved away to take his seat at the head of the table with a grim look. Melinda sat next to her grandmother, who presided at the opposite end of the table from Robert.

Over the top of a lovely white rose centerpiece, Ellie saw Constance for the first time that evening, across the table. She looked years younger in an off-the-shoulder satin gown of emerald green, which suited her complexion...and matched the color of Robert's eyes. Constance caught Ellie's eye and nodded with a small smile. Ellie saw her look to Robert and then back at Ellie again. She gave the dark-haired beauty a toothy grin and dropped her gaze to fiddle with her linen napkin. When she raised her eyes again, Constance was deep in conversation with the attractive silver-haired gentleman who'd escorted Mrs. Chamberlain in to dinner.

"Well, this is most fortunate, Ellie. How could I have been so lucky?"

Ellie turned toward her right to see Stephen sliding into the chair next to her. She smiled in relief. Now she wouldn't have to try to converse with a stranger.

"Oh, I'm glad you're sitting here."

"Why, thank you, Ellie. I am flattered."

She blushed. "Oh, you know what I mean. It's just

that I don't know anyone here, and I've already met you, so..."

Stephen chuckled and nodded. "Just so. I feel exactly the same way."

Ellie found herself in the difficult position of either having to lock her eyes on Stephen or occasionally glance past him down the table to see Robert watching her with narrowed eyes and a deepened cleft in his chin as he frowned.

"Ummm...what do you do, Stephen...for a living?"

"My family has some holdings in Seattle, so I am blessed such that I do not have to work. I teach history at the University on occasion."

Previously distracted by Robert's continued glares, Ellie did lock eyes on Stephen at that.

"Really? I teach college."

Stephen's eyes widened, and he sat back to study her. "You, Ellie? A college professor?"

"Well, I'm not a professor. Adjunct faculty, actually."

"I did not know women..." He raised his eyebrows. "Chicago has certainly taken some unusual steps in their educational system."

Ellie knew she'd made a mistake, given women's roles at the turn of the century, but she tried to bluster through.

"How so, Stephen?"

"Well, I...em...I have never heard of a female teaching at the college level."

"Oh, really?" Ellie moved into her drawl. "But you make it sound farfetched...an improbability."

He blushed. "Oh, no, far be it from me to judge. No, I think it is an excellent idea."

Ellie couldn't keep her eyes from Robert. He had turned away to speak to an older woman at his side.

"Do you teach home economics, then?"

Ellie narrowed her eyes and regarded him. He was growing less attractive by the moment.

"No, like you, I teach history. Women's studies."

"Women's studies? I have never heard of such a class. What would a class like that entail? What sort of material might you cover?"

Ellie sighed. She had to give the man a break. He

103

was just another turn-of-the-century kind of guy.

"Women, Stephen," she spoke patiently. "We study women. The contribution of women in history and society."

"Oh," he murmured with the grace to blush. "Forgive me, Ellie, I did not mean to sound...boorish. It is just that I have never heard of such a curriculum."

"I'm sure a lot of people haven't. It's fairly new." Ellie snuck another look at Robert, who had downed his second glass of wine, by her count. Good gravy, was the man an alcoholic? He met her eyes over the rim of her glass, his narrow gaze cool and distant.

She dropped her eyes and welcomed the arrival of the first course.

Course after course arrived. Cook had prepared a few things especially for Ellie, and she soon found herself full of food, in part due to the tightness of the dress. Stephen spoke of benign matters such as Seattle and the university; she listened with half an ear while she watched Robert. Occasionally, she turned and caught glimpses of Constance, apparently deep in conversation with her silver-haired neighbor.

While Stephen was occupied with his companion to the right, Ellie looked down the table at Mrs. Chamberlain, who caught her eye and gave her a reserved nod. Seated next to Mrs. Chamberlain was a terrified-looking James. He wore the look of a trapped animal as he stared at Melinda across the table to her grandmother's right.

In between courses, Ellie found time to greet the young girl on her left, who seemed as shy as Ellie felt. They smiled at one another in recognition and left the conversation at that, relaxed and silent as they surveyed the room or picked at their food.

When the twelve-course dinner ended, the guests returned to the drawing room, where chairs and tables had been rearranged to allow for dancing. A trio of string players was warming up in a corner of the room.

Stephen had offered Ellie his arm following dinner and now led her to a seat near the wall.

"Oh, I couldn't sit. I'd better stand. I ate too much," she murmured as she patted her stomach. She kept a watchful eye out for Robert, who had not yet entered the room.

Out of the corner of her eye, Ellie saw Stephen blink in surprise at her comments. She realized with a twinge of guilt that she needed to make more of an attempt to conform to the customs of the day...especially simple ones in etiquette and language. She was sufficiently well read on the era to avoid making huge mistakes, but some mischievous part of her insisted on acting as if she were in the twenty-first century. For now, only Robert knew of her origins...what little they both knew.

"Sorry. I'm a bit outspoken," she murmured.

"Not at all," Stephen said gallantly. "I find your forthrightness quite refreshing."

Ellie dragged her eyes from a search for Robert long enough to meet Stephen's sincere gaze. He certainly was a nice man, she thought wistfully. Seemingly uncomplicated and honest. Relaxing. Safe.

Robert entered the room at that moment accompanying the older woman with whom he'd been seated. Ellie watched with admiration as he bent his dark head toward the woman, who literally batted her eyelashes at her handsome escort.

She sighed and bit her lip, with a pang of remorse. She had treated him poorly before dinner, forgetting that she took of his generosity by staying in his home, eating his food and wearing his sister's clothing.

Still, wasn't it all just a dream, she wondered? Did she need to worry about the niceties? About pretending to be from this era? What did it matter, if she was going to disappear soon anyway? Time travel, indeed! Didn't there have to be a catalyst, some angst, or at least a machine, to facilitate such a journey?

Robert seated the woman on a green velvet settee across the room, next to his grandmother, then lifted his head and met Ellie's eyes for a brief moment. Her heart began to pound in her throat, and she wondered if he could see the surprise in her eyes as she realized she'd fallen in love. She tried to smile, but her lips refused to do more than lift at one corner. Robert dropped his eyes and made his way over to the musicians.

"Ellie, did you hear me?"

Ellie came back to reality at the sound of Stephen's voice. She turned to him in a daze.

"I'm sorry. What?"

"I asked if you would like to dance. The musicians appear to have warmed up, and the music should begin momentarily. I do not normally dance, but I would be pleased if you would honor me."

His face finally came into focus as she let go of a green-eyed image. "What? Dance?" She turned toward the musicians who indeed were rubbing bows across willing strings. "Oh, Stephen, I don't know how. I can't."

Stephen took her hand in his warm, reassuring grasp and tucked it into his arm.

"Neither one of us does, so we will just muddle as best we can out there." He led her away from the wall and toward the center of the room. Ellie looked around in a panic, the blur of faces seeming to stare only at her. Melinda came to dance with an extremely tall James. A young, redheaded man led her friend Amy onto the floor.

Ellie had visions of standing in the middle of the floor, completely ignorant of the steps to some intricate quadrille, while onlookers stared and whispered. Stephen opened his arms as any twenty-first century man might, and Ellie went into them. He began to move her around the floor in a modified waltz suitable for the size of the room. For all his protestations, Stephen danced with a smooth, elegant style, and Ellie relaxed into his arms.

Over his shoulder, she saw a grim-faced Robert lead a glowing Constance onto the floor. He glanced at Ellie once without expression and looked away. She dropped her eyes to Stephen's shoulder, hating the jealousy that hit her with a wave of nausea. She'd only met Robert two days ago...if they'd really ever met at all. She was engaged—to Kyle. Robert would have a life of his own...without her. She reminded herself as she had reminded Robert. She was just passing through. It seemed quite likely that she would wake up in the morning—or in an hour—and Robert would be the fleeting whisper of a dream she couldn't remember in the light of day.

"We are doing very well together, Ellie. You are making me look like a very accomplished dancer."

Ellie looked up to see Stephen smiling. She'd almost forgotten where she was.

"Yes, we do dance well together, don't we, Stephen? I didn't know what everyone was dancing these days."

"I take it you have not been out in public much lately, then?"

She peeked over his shoulder to watch Robert and Constance. *They* danced well together, with an ease of familiarity. It seemed likely they had danced before.

"Ellie?"

She returned her preoccupied gaze to Stephen's kind eyes.

"Yes? No. I mean, no, I don't usually dance, so... I don't know how you managed to get me out here." She smiled at him weakly.

"By sheer force, Ellie. I manhandled you out here, but it is working very nicely, I think."

She managed to return his grin but found her eyes straying toward Robert once again.

The dance ended, and Stephen returned Ellie to her position by the wall, apparently intent on remaining by her side, for which she was grateful. He nodded to acquaintances and introduced Ellie, giving her more insight on who they were once they'd moved on. A lively dance ensued, and Ellie watched the younger people frolic on the floor. Robert remained glued to Constance's side, his head bent to hear her every word, an occasional smile lighting his face.

Ellie continued to feel sick to her stomach, with an ache near her chest. She suspected it might be heartburn...or something.

"Stephen, you'll have to forgive me. I'm really not feeling well. I think I'm going to have to go upstairs."

He turned to her with concern. "Ellie, I am sorry to hear that. Is there anything I can do? Should I call someone? Melinda, perhaps?"

She shook her head vehemently. She just wanted to sneak out and disappear.

"No, no, thank you. It was very nice to meet you. I hope I see you again soon."

Stephen caught her hand as she turned away. "And you, Ellie. I hope to see you again soon." In a surprise move, he brought her hand to his lips and pressed a kiss on the back.

Ellie caught her breath at the bold move and dipped into a teensy curtsy with downcast eyes before she moved out of the room. Her plan to hurry up the stairs was thwarted by having to drag her gown with her, but she made it to her room in good time. Unwilling to call Alice to help her get out of the dress, Ellie dropped onto the bed face first. Whatever she'd been holding in released itself, because she promptly burst into tears and sobbed into the quilt.

A firm knock on her door penetrated her consciousness, and she clamped her mouth shut and held her breath, hoping whoever it was would go away. Another knock followed. Ellie sighed. It was probably Melinda or Alice come to check on her. She tussled and struggled with her voluminous gown and unyielding corset to throw herself off the bed and move toward the door, opening it at last to find Robert with his hand raised, ready to knock again.

"Is everything all right? Are you ill?" The concern in his voice threatened to send her off into another crying spell.

Ellie dashed a hand across her face, hoping he couldn't see her tears in the muted light of the hall.

"No, I'm fine. I must have eaten something that disagreed with me. I-I apologize for leaving without saying anything."

"Well, apparently you thought it important enough to advise Mr. Sadler of your poor health." His eyes hardened as he gazed at her.

"What?" she mumbled, confused and miserably unhappy. What had happened to the carefree man she'd met only two days ago?

"I am afraid I found it necessary to ask your constant companion, Mr. Sadler, where you had gone, and he was so kind as to tell me that you felt ill."

"Oh." She shook her head and rolled her eyes. "I said I was sorry, Robert. I didn't think anyone would miss me. You seemed...occupied."

"Well, you thought wrong. Do you need a physician?" He clasped his hands behind his back and searched her face.

She shook her head. "No, I'm fine. You should probably return to your guests. I'm sure Constance would like to see you." She hated her snide remark.

"Yes, I am sure she would," he said without a blink. Ellie's heart sank. "Very well, then. I shall leave you to rest. I will send Alice up to help you."

"No, thank you, Robert. I hate to bother your employees at night. I can undress by myself."

"If you could, you would be out of that dress by now. I was not unaware of how uncomfortable you looked this evening."

"Me?" She looked at him in surprise. "Actually, the dress is quite comfortable now that I am used to it."

"Oh! I thought...you looked unhappy." His eyes softened, and his tight mouth relaxed for a moment.

"I-I'm...fine. I do apologize for being so rude to you earlier. I must seem very ungrateful, after all you have done for me."

He shook his head firmly. "There is no need to apologize. I was rude, as well. I was not myself. If you will not have Alice, is there anything I can do for you?"

Ellie thought about asking him to take her in his arms and lay with her for the rest of the night...or even for the rest of her life. Then she recovered from the moment of insanity.

"Noooo. Well, yes, actually, there is." She swallowed hard. He would turn her down flat.

"What is it?"

"I wonder...if you could...umm...unzip this dress. After that, I'll be fine, really. It's just I can't reach." Having asked the question, Ellie wished the earth would swallow her up. The shocked expression on Robert's face tore through her heart. She hadn't exactly asked the man to make love to her...as she wanted.

"Oh, I-I'm sorry. I can see you're shocked. Never mind, I can do this. I'll be fine. Forget I asked." Ellie grabbed the door to shut it, but he put out his hand to block it.

"No, no, that is fine. I am not shocked. At least, I do not think I am. Turn around."

Ellie obediently turned. Nothing happened for a long,

long moment, and she looked over her shoulder.

"Is everything all right? Can you see the zipper?"

He cleared his throat, but when he spoke, it sounded husky.

"Em...yes, I am fine. Just a moment."

Ellie felt his hand flat against her back as he used his other to unzip the dress. The zipper seemed overly long because it took him a long time to lower it. She grabbed the front of the dress to keep it on. Her neck and back tingled to his touch. If he would just press his body against her, she would be the happiest woman in the world. She almost willed it, but he cleared his throat once again and moved away. She could tell by the sudden coolness on her back. She stepped behind the door and turned, peeking out from the side.

"Thank you. I appreciate it. I'll see you in the morning."

Robert stared hard at her, his hand still in midair. He seemed at a loss for a moment. He dropped his hand and cleared his throat once again.

"Yes, yes, of course. You are welcome. Good night, then."

"Good night," she murmured, closing the door on the man she wanted above all others. Unwilling to let him go, she pressed her face against the wood, listening for his footsteps. A full minute passed before she heard his soft step on the carpet as he moved down the hall toward the stairs.

With a sigh, she turned away from the door and crossed to the bed. She wriggled out of the dress and petticoats and slipped the soft white linen nightgown over her head. Alice had laid out a matching robe, but Ellie tossed that onto the chair before she climbed into the bed. She burrowed into the covers and pressed her face into a pillow.

Her chest still ached, and she realized it wasn't heartburn. She now knew where the word heartache came from. It really did hurt. The deeper she fell under the Victorian man's spell, the more awkward things became. If this was a dream, why couldn't she control its outcome? Was he in love with Constance? Would he marry someday? Why couldn't she awaken when it became too painful?

She closed her eyes and willed sleep to come, but it took its sweet time arriving.

****

Ellie opened her eyes to a sliver of gray light coming through the curtains. She turned over and looked at her clock. 5:57 a.m. The alarm would go off in a few minutes. She stared at it again drowsily, aware of an intense feeling of sadness. Her dreams! She must have been dreaming. Ellie squeezed her eyes shut in an effort to recall the dream, to locate the source of the strange grief that ached in her throat. A sense of loss, green eyes, a warm hand on her back. The elusive memory escaped her, and she sighed. She pushed a button on the clock to turn it off and turned over.

Kyle faced her, snoring lightly, his blonde hair ruffled like a little boy's mop. She studied his face. Perennially young, it seemed as if he would never age. At thirty-five, he had no wrinkles, no sun damage, no worry lines. She sighed softly. He hardly ever worried. Life seemed to happen around him but not to him. She wondered how they'd ever managed to stay together, given her inability to control her emotions, and his inability to emote. Inability or unwillingness—she never knew.

His blue eyes drifted open, and he stared at her for a moment.

"Good morning," she murmured.

"Morning," he said as he turned over, leaving Ellie to stare at the back of his tousled head. She'd hoped for a good-morning kiss, at the least, though that was not their custom. In fact, Kyle had just done what he did every morning, turn over and go back to sleep for a few minutes while she dressed.

She wished he would look intently into her eyes just once, but she couldn't remember him ever looking intently at anything other than the newspaper. She sighed and crawled out of bed to head for the shower. Fifteen minutes later, she gently shook his shoulder to wake him. Moving to her closet, she dragged out the nearest sweater and skirt and slipped the one over her shoulders and the other over her hips. She paused as she stared at the zipper, a memory tugging at her subconscious, along with the oddest thought that getting dressed had been particularly easy this morning.

Kyle rolled out of bed and stepped into the shower. Ellie made her way into the kitchen and turned on the coffeepot. Kyle liked to have his coffee ready when he woke. She poured herself a cup of orange juice and looked at her watch. No time to drink it. She'd have to fly out of the apartment to catch the El to the college. She grabbed her purse and headed for the door.

"See ya, Kyle."

"Wait, Ellie." Kyle rushed into the living room, still wet from his shower, a towel wrapped around his waist. Ellie turned back in surprise. "Wait," he murmured as he dashed back into the bedroom. He emerged in a moment, wearing a robe.

"I have to go, Kyle. Can this wait?"

"No. No, Ellie, it can't. I've been waiting for a while now."

Ellie stared at him, normally such a calm man, now nervously clanking in the kitchen for a coffee cup. She held her bag and waited.

"Sit down," he mumbled as he moved toward the breakfast table.

"Ummm...okay." She pulled out a seat and perched on the edge. "What's going on?"

Kyle stared down into his cup for a moment and then glanced at her across the table. His eyes flickered around the room; he couldn't seem to keep them steady. He resumed his study of his coffee.

"Kyle? I have to go." Ellie was going to miss the train, and she would be late. It didn't really matter. She didn't have an early class, but she did have papers to read and grade.

"I know. I know. Wait just a minute." He put up a hand and took a deep breath. "Ellie, I don't know how to say this to you, but...I...I'm moving out."

Ellie dropped her purse. "What?"

"I've met someone. I'm sorry. I hate to do this to you. We've been together so long."

"But how...I thought...we were going—"

"I know. I know." He couldn't keep his eyes on her

face. "I know we were going to get married, but we've never set a date. *You* never set a date."

"*Me*? What about you?" Confusion more than anything reigned supreme in Ellie's mind. She assumed the shock of the moment trumped everything and that misery and grief would soon follow, but for now she just felt confused.

"Okay," he raised a pacifying hand. "Neither one of us set a date." He finally managed to meet her eyes. "Doesn't that tell you something?"

She shook her head and remained silent. He was right. She'd felt more of a sense of loss when she'd awakened from her dreams.

"I-I don't know what to say. Are you in love with her?"

Kyle blinked for a moment and nodded sheepishly. "Yeah, I think I am." He raised a hand to his forehead and rubbed it. Then his eyes flickered back to her face again. "I always loved you, Ellie. You have to know that."

Ellie smiled weakly. "I know, Kyle. I know. I loved you, too." It seemed they'd said all they could. She rose once again, trying to remember what her morning routine was. Go out the door, catch the El, go to work. "I still love you," she murmured in a daze.

Kyle moved toward her, unexpectedly pulling her into his arms in an unusual gesture of affection.

"I still love you, too, Ellie. I'm sorry." He pressed her face against his chest. He smelled of soap, his scent familiar, recognizable.

She pulled away, tears in her eyes. "When? When are you leaving?"

He hung his head for a moment before he looked up. "Today. I'll be gone before you get home."

Ellie caught her breath. "So soon? I-I didn't know it would be so soon. Why?"

"I think it's best, Ellie."

"Are you...are you going to move in with her?" Ellie knew she shouldn't ask but she couldn't help herself. The future looked bleak. While their relationship lacked spontaneity and romance, he had been her companion...the man she'd expected to marry, until a few short moments ago.

Kyle studied the carpet for a moment. "Ellie, I don't think you want to know."

She bit her lip and turned away in humiliation. "You're right. I don't want to know." She hurried toward the door before the tears fell onto her face. "I have to go."

"Ellie," he called, but she did not turn back.

Chapter Eleven

Ellie woke up in the dark—disoriented, confused. She turned to look at her clock but couldn't see the bright blue numbers. She rolled over onto her other side and put out a hand. The rest of the bed was empty and cold. No Kyle. He was gone!

A sliver of light peeped under the door, and she crawled out of bed to make her way toward the faint glow. She pulled open the door and peeked out. A soft light from a wall sconce kept the darkness of the hallway at bay. She was back in the Queen Anne house again. But in what era? What if she'd slipped back into the dream in another time? What if Robert no longer lived? Had she dreamt about Kyle? Was she dreaming now? The alternative—time travel—was just not possible.

Ellie turned back and grabbed her robe from the chair. She tiptoed into the hallway and shut the door behind her with a small click, unwilling to wake Melinda just down the hall...if she was still there.

Ellie made her way to the staircase, gripped the banister tightly, and followed it down, one careful step at a time. The darkened foyer revealed nothing. A round table stood in the middle...as it had. She ran her hand along the sleek wood, but couldn't tell if the table was the same.

The first floor lay in darkness except for a sliver of light under the study door. She moved toward it and rested her ear against the wood, listening for sounds. The last thing she wanted was to wake up in the house with a complete set of strangers. Ellie found the handle, eased open the door and peeked in.

A small lamp on an occasional table provided the only light in the room. Robert slumped in one of the easy chairs—jacket and tie discarded, his normally well-groomed hair disheveled, an empty wineglass in his hand. A bottle of wine sat on the carpet at his feet. The scene, though at odds with the controlled man she thought she knew, brought her an intense feeling of relief. She had not lost him forever...not yet.

"Robert," she whispered, unsure if he slept.

His eyes popped open, and he turned in her direction. He struggled to rise.

"Ellie, what are you doing here? Are you ill?"

He moved toward her, his hand outstretched. In the soft light of the room, she found courage and reached for his hand.

"No, I feel all right. I had a dream. I thought I had returned to my own time. Or maybe I'm dreaming now. I was so scared I wouldn't see you again." Ellie's voice broke as she looked up into his haggard face.

Robert pulled her into his arms and buried his face in her neck, holding her tightly to him. Taken completely by surprise, she froze for a moment. His breath against her neck made her knees weak. She tilted her head back to look at him for a moment. Was he drunk? This was so unlike the seemingly proper turn-of-the-century man she'd met.

Robert stared down into her face with troubled eyes. He cupped her face in his hands and bent his head to kiss her. At the first warm touch of his lips on hers, he slid his arms around her once again and held her as if he would never let her go.

Delirious with the unexpected pleasure of his spontaneous kiss, Ellie wrapped her arms around his neck and rose up on tiptoe in an effort to mold herself to his body. She kissed him with abandon...without reserve. The past, present and future came together in a passionate crescendo as she moved against him. She felt him respond to her, pulling her tighter and tighter against him until she couldn't breathe. His hands roamed her back until his hand caught in her hair.

Then he stilled suddenly and put Ellie from him. Unable to stop herself, she reached for him again, but he placed gentle hands on her shoulders. In the soft light of the study, she saw that his eyes traveled the length of her body as no well-bred Victorian man should allow. She blushed. What was he thinking? That she had no morals, no self-control?

"Ellie, we cannot." His breathing was ragged. "I cannot tell you how much I want you, but I will not take advantage of you."

"Yes, you can." Ellie heard the words she wanted. He wanted her. She moved toward him again. With a groan, he pulled her to him. Still, he held back. With one hand under her chin, he raised her face to his. He gazed into her eyes and shook his head.

"No, this is not right. I am drunk. I have had the most difficult night. You are a guest in my house with few resources. I will not compromise you."

Ellie grinned. He'd gone Victorian on her. She couldn't believe he'd actually said *compromise*. How cute!

"Robert, I forgive you for being drunk. You are no less appealing to me. I choose to come to you willingly. You could never *compromise* me. I'm a twenty-first-century woman. We don't get *compromised* anymore."

Still, he held back, refusing to do more than hold her against him and bury his face in her hair.

"We did not have an opportunity to dance this evening," he murmured in her ear.

Ellie tilted her head back to look at him. "Were you going to dance with me tonight? I couldn't tell."

Even in the soft light, she could see the deep dimples above his grin. "Of course I was going to dance with you...if Sadler could be persuaded to leave your side for a moment."

Ellie snorted. "You mean if you could tear yourself away from Constance long enough."

He pulled her against him more tightly. She struggled to breathe but relished the moment.

"Nonsense. Let's dance."

Ellie looked around the fully furnished and carpeted study. "Here? Now?"

"Yes, here and now." Robert kept hold of her with one hand and raised his other arm. Ellie slid her hand into his palm. He stepped out and began to move her around the room in a graceful waltz. She followed him effortlessly, prancing around the room in her bare feet on the carpet, two or three steps to his every one. Though no music accompanied their dance, a symphony played in Ellie's head. She began to hum a tune as Robert twirled her around the furniture. As she laughed and responded to his charming grin, she felt heady, carefree, romantic and very much in love. The dreamy dance ended when Ellie stubbed her toe on a leg of the desk.

"Ouch," she mumbled, grabbing her foot, hopping.

"Oh, my dear, I am so sorry," Robert chuckled. He led her over to his chair and pulled her down onto his lap. He held her while they examined the toe together under the lamp, but no bones appeared to be broken. When she made as if to rise, he held her against him.

"Well, don't you think this is a bit compromising?" She relaxed into his arms but arched an eyebrow.

He grinned. "Yes, I do, but I cannot help myself." He raised her hand and brought it to her lips.

A book on the small table, next to his wineglass, caught her eye. She peered at it closely.

"You're reading the H. G. Wells book, Robert."

He stared at it for a moment. "Yes."

"Is that a coincidence? Did you conjure me up with a time machine?"

Robert failed to respond to her joke. He eased her off his lap and jumped up to pace the room restlessly. Ellie knew a moment of desolation. She hugged herself. Robert noticed and took both her hands.

"I am looking for answers," he murmured as he pulled her into his arms again.

"Answers to what, Robert? What?"

"To tell me how to keep you here. How to keep you with me." His husky voice tore at her heart. "I-I have written a letter to Mr. Wells to discuss some of his thoughts on time travel. I do not expect a response for weeks, but I hope he will give me some encouragement."

Ellie leaned back to stare at him. "Robert, you didn't tell him about me, did you?"

He laughed without humor. "Do you think I am mad, woman? No, no, I did not discuss your...ah...arrival with him. I asked if he believed time travel was possible...and that if one traveled in time...could the traveler stay in the time or would they have to return." He cleared his throat. "I asked other things, but that was the gist of the letter."

Ellie touched the side of his face tenderly. "Robert, I didn't come in a machine...other than the train. It's not the same thing."

He pulled away from her to pace the room once again. "I know, I know. But perhaps Mr. Wells used the machine with literary license. Perhaps it was just an acceptable metaphor for something we do not yet understand."

Ellie watched him as he wandered the room, restlessly placing one hand on his hip and the other to the back of his neck or alternatively clasping both hands behind his back. The man seemed possessed with finding an answer to something she thought she already knew. It was a dream. And in the dream, he was in pain...because of her. The happy-go-lucky, charming, suave man had evolved into a grim-faced, unhappy and morose man seized by doubts and confused by a phenomenon neither of them understood.

She sank into a chair and watched him stalk about the room.

"Robert, come here. Please sit down," she called. He stopped pacing and returned to the chair beside her.

"What is it, my love?"

Her heart soared at the endearment, but she tightened her lips against the romantic aura his words evoked. He'd known her for only a couple of days. How could he be in love? She ignored the fact that she herself had fallen fast and hard.

"I can't stand to see you like this, Robert. You look miserable. If this is my doing, then I need to fix it."

Robert reached for her hand and brought it to his lips, turning it over to kiss the inside of her wrist. His mouth felt warm and delicious on the tender, exposed skin. Against the responding stirrings in her body, Ellie held fast to her thoughts.

"Do you hear me, Robert? I need to fix it."

"And how would you do that, Ellie?" he murmured as he kept her hand in his. "Can you guarantee me that you will not disappear? Can you promise me that the future will not snatch you away again? Can you assure me that I am not some poor sap in a dream of your making?"

She shook her head mutely.

Robert rose from his chair and pulled her back into his arms.

"I cannot bear to lose you, Ellie, not now that I have found you. I have waited so long for you. I do not care whether this is a dream or if you have traveled through time to come to me. I do not want you to wake up one morning and forget me. I do not want you to disappear."

Ellie shivered at his words, though her heart craved the love he so eloquently expressed. His fear and pain seemed genuine, and she knew she must make a decision. It could not go on. But for now...just for now...she would forget the future.

"Stay with me then, Robert. Don't let me go to sleep. I'm terrified that I'll wake up and you'll be gone...that I'll be taken from you."

He whispered against her hair. "Hush, my love. I will stay with you. I will not let you go." He lowered himself into the chair and pulled her down into her arms, cradling her on his lap like a child. "I have waited all my life to fall in love. I will not lose you now."

They stayed together for hours, without words, without movement. Ellie rest her face on his chest and listened to the rhythm of his heart. How could such a strong, steady heartbeat belong to a shadowy figure in a dream? She fell asleep toward dawn.

****

Robert did not sleep. It was an impossibility with Ellie in his arms. While she slept, he studied her face and her body, longing to trace a line from her eyes to her lips with his fingers. He barely suppressed the urge to caress the soft curves of her thinly dressed figure. It was all he could do not to stroke the sleek curls of the dark hair that dangled over his arm.

But he did not want to awaken her, and he chose to do nothing but watch her—committing her face to memory...in case the worst came to pass. He drew in a deep breath and released it, gritting his teeth as he contemplated losing her. He was determined that would not happen this night. He would not let it. He would hold Ellie against him until dawn, securely in his arms. She would not slip away from him through time or in a dream. Not on this night.

****

Ellie made her way to her room early in the morning,

after Robert kissed her and told her he had to go work. She looked around her room and wished things could have been different, but they weren't. Robert's safe and secure life had turned upside down. He was miserable and uncertain of the future, and it was her fault. She would take action.

She found paper and pen...not a ballpoint but the old kind, with metal nib and ink...in the drawer of the nightstand, and she wrote out a note. When Alice came to help her dress, she gave her the note and asked her to have it delivered immediately. Alice left with the letter, and Ellie waited in her room. She couldn't face the rest of the house. Melinda would probably sleep in, and Mrs. Chamberlain always took breakfast in her room.

Two hours passed, and still Ellie heard nothing. She tried to think of mom's apple pie and the boy next door while she waited for a response. What if an answer never came? What if she had exposed her plans only to have them betrayed?

Alice tapped on the door.

"Mrs. Green is here to see you, ma'am."

Ellie jumped up. Constance! She headed down the stairs, tripping occasionally on the green skirt Alice had managed to squeeze her into earlier that morning.

Alice followed her down and opened the door to the parlor. Ellie slid in and shut the door behind her quietly.

Constance stood at the window, gazing down on the view of the city below. Her dark blue tailor-made silk suit and jacket showed her slim figure off to perfection, the netted hat giving her a regal bearing Ellie knew she could never hope to achieve.

"Constance, thank you for coming. May I offer you some tea?" Some well-trained servant had thoughtfully placed a tea tray on the mahogany table in front of the sofa.

"No, thank you, Ellie. Your note sounded urgent. Is everything all right? How can I help?"

Now that Constance had arrived, Ellie's grand scheme suddenly looked foolish.

"If you don't mind, I think I'll just have a cup. Are you sure?"

Constance looked at her curiously and acquiesced.

They sipped tea for a few minutes while Ellie composed her chaotic thoughts.

"I need your help, Constance."

"Yes, so you said in your note."

Ellie's face burned. She had to be insane asking a stranger for help.

"I'm sorry to trouble you, but I don't know many people here."

Constance tilted her head. "You know Robert."

"Yes, well, that's just it. This is about Robert."

Out of the corner of her eye, Ellie saw Constance stiffen.

"I see," she murmured.

"Oh, no, it's not what you think, Constance. You see, I need to *leave* the house. Then I'll be out of your hair and out of Robert's hair."

"*My* hair. Whatever do you mean, Ellie?" Two bright spots of color shown on Constance's pale skin.

Ellie turned a frank look on her. "You know what I mean, Constance. It's obvious that you have a crush on Robert...that is...that you care for him. That's what I mean by *out of your hair*."

Constance dropped her cup onto her saucer and put the cup down. "I-I...well, I... Is it that obvious?" she murmured.

"It is to me. I share the same problem as you."

"You are saying that you too...em...care for him?"

Ellie drew in a deep breath and released it. She nodded. "Yes, I do. I think I'm in love. So you see, we are both in the same boat."

From the shocked look on Constance's face, Ellie thought the dark-haired beauty was going to jump up and stalk out of the room, but she tightened her lips and stayed in place...her eyebrows raised in inquiry.

"Ellie, I do not know why you are here or where you really came from. I must be frank. I wish that you were not here. Since you first appeared, Robert has hardly spoken two words to me. I thought he and I were close friends. In fact, I hoped..." She picked up her tea again and studied the inside of the cup.

"You hoped that he would ask you to marry him?" Ellie knew she took a chance with the woman's good graces.

Constance threw Ellie a quick, self-conscious look and nodded.

"Yes," she whispered. "I did."

Ellie stared down at the light blue oriental carpeting, fighting an unexpected blast from her own jealous furnace. Constance hadn't revealed anything Ellie didn't already know, but to hear her say it aloud... She took a deep breath.

"Well, you might still get your chance. As I mentioned, I need to leave the house, and it should be in such a way that Robert knows I'm okay but doesn't know where I am."

"Why?" Constance asked bluntly. She narrowed her eyes and watched Ellie's face closely.

Ellie colored. "I-I have outstayed my welcome. Robert and his family have been very kind to me, but I can't live off their generosity forever. The truth is...I-I'm not staying in Seattle. I will be leaving soon, though I'm not sure when. I-I'm just waiting on a letter from my parents. They'll send word when they are settled in their new house and I can return home." Ellie could hardly keep up with her convoluted lie, but she did the best she could with little sleep and a heart that ached.

"I see," said Constance though her puzzled face showed that she clearly did not.

"I know it doesn't make sense right now. So difficult to explain. My parents. Such odd creatures, really." Ellie babbled on till she was out of breath.

"And how can I help you, Ellie?"

"I need to find a boarding house. I have a piece of jewelry that I need help selling so I can pay for my room."

Constance drew in a deep breath and stared into the distance.

"This sounds so...irregular, Ellie. Are you sure? Have you ever been to a rooming house?"

"No, but I've read about them. I was hoping you could find a suitable one...perhaps one for working women." A small smile broke through. "If I have to stay here long, I'll have to go to work, so..."

"Work? What could you do?"

"I can teach, Constance. I am a teacher by

profession."

"Really? How interesting. Yes, now that you mention it, I do recall a boarding house for professional women. My next-door neighbor has a sister who runs such a house. I will make inquiries right away. When do you need to leave?"

Ellie swallowed hard. "Today, right now."

Constance turned to stare. "Ellie, that is impossible. What has happened to make you run from this house? Are you in trouble? Did Robert—"

"No, no, nothing like that, Constance." Ellie's face flamed. "I simply need to leave. I hope you understand. If you are as hopelessly in love with Robert as I am, you'll understand."

To Ellie's surprise, Constance shook her head. "In this situation, I do not understand. I enjoy Robert's company very much, but I have not been *hopelessly in love* since my husband died." She paused and stared into the distance with a small smile. "I loved him like no other." She returned her gaze to Ellie. "I care for Robert a great deal. He was very kind to me when my husband died, but I am not madly in love with him."

"Oh," Ellie murmured...momentarily stumped. How was that possible? Who wouldn't be madly in love with a charming, arrogant, kind, rash, affectionate, debonair man with laughing eyes like Robert?

"I did hope to marry again some day, and Robert would make a very suitable husband, but..." She quirked a wry eyebrow in Ellie's direction. "I think his interests lie elsewhere."

Ellie swallowed hard. Another wave of color heated her cheeks. "Well, not with me, that's for sure. We hardly know each other...and as I said, I'm going to be leaving at some time in the near future. I don't think it would be right to continue to live off his largesse, as it were."

"I understand. From what I know of Robert, he does need a woman who is willing to stay with him. It is a shame that you cannot move to Seattle permanently."

Ellie bit her lips. "Oh, well, you know. My duty lies with my parents. They need me."

"I understand." Constance rose. "Well, I have much to do if I am to find you rooms before the end of the day.

What is the jewelry that you will be selling? I do not think you will need the money today, but you might need some pin money by tomorrow, if you are to be on your own."

Ellie pulled a ribbon out from beneath the high lace collar of her shirtwaist blouse and showed Constance the white-gold diamond engagement ring on it.

Constance gasped, wide-eyed. "Oh, my word. I have never seen such a beautiful ring. It must be worth a fortune."

Ellie chuckled. "Not really, but I hope I can get a reasonable amount for it."

"It almost looks like... Is that an engagement ring, Ellie?"

Ellie grimaced. "It was."

"I had no idea."

"It is over."

"Oh!" Constance replied. "I am sorry to hear that. Well, we can take it to a pawn shop tomorrow. For now, I must hurry. If I am able to obtain a room for you, I will send a note to you with the address. I will meet you there."

Ellie reached to hug the taller woman. "Thank you, Constance. Thank you! I can't tell you how much I appreciate this."

"Of course, Ellie. I will have the carriage wait for you when I send the note." She left the room like a woman with a mission, and Ellie felt infinitely better than she had all morning.

She returned to her room and waited for news. While she waited, she considered her situation. She could not possibly take Melinda's clothing, and yet she really couldn't walk around unnoticed in her oversized sweater, denim skirt and clogs. In addition, she had to say goodbye to Melinda and Mrs. Chamberlain...and Robert.

Ellie sat down and pulled out paper and the irritating pen that dripped blotches of ink all over her letters. She penned a thank-you note to Mrs. Chamberlain, a more sincere and affectionate note to Melinda telling her she would have to borrow at least one set of clothes until she could obtain her own, and a final note to Robert—that broke her heart and set her to sobbing—with words that seemed trite and contrived.

How could she tell him she was leaving because she was in love? How could she explain she thought it best to remove herself from his existence now, while he was merely infatuated with the thought of a time traveler and before they grew closer? Before she disappeared back to the waking world or her own time? How could she say he needed to get on with a life based in reality...as did she?

Her reasons for leaving seemed foolish when written down, but she was as sure as she'd ever been in her life that she had to go. She loved him too much to have him wake up one morning to find her gone. Ellie squashed the inconvenient thought that, if all went as planned, he would simply come home that day and find her gone.

After several false starts and crumpled pieces of paper, she finally decided on the best approach to make him forget about her. She told him she was engaged!

She left the letters on the dressing table, knowing one of the maids would find them later. Noon had come and gone. A carriage pulled up, and Ellie peeked out the window, expecting to see a messenger with a note. She panicked when she saw Robert descending. Having made her decision to go, she could not face him. He might come looking for her. She ran to the door and locked it. How would she get out of the house without his knowledge? He would surely hear a carriage arrive.

Ellie pressed her head against the door and waited. She heard footsteps in the hallway. They paused at her door for a moment. She felt sure he would hear the pounding of her heart through the thick wood. She held her breath. An eternity seemed to pass in a few moments, and then he moved on down the hall to his own room.

Ellie tiptoed away from the door and peeked outside the window. She had no choice. She would have to make a run for it when the carriage came. Hopefully, the messenger would have good news. Otherwise, she'd look quite the fool jumping into a carriage only to be tossed right back out onto the street.

An hour passed. She heard Melinda's voice in the hallway, a whispered conversation with Alice, and then silence as Melinda descended the stairs. Ellie crept back to the window again. Melinda and her grandmother climbed into the carriage. She wondered where they were going. Perhaps to someone's house for tea. Ellie thanked her lucky stars for having the foresight to tell Alice that she was feeling ill and would keep to her room.

Ellie bundled her clothes together and continued to wait. She heard the thud of horse's hooves and the jingle of a carriage's livery. She looked down again. A strange carriage. A short man stepped down from his seat beside the driver, an envelope in his hand.

This was it! Ellie grabbed her things, pulled open the door and dashed down the stairs. She reached the front door before the messenger knocked and startled him by swinging open the door, grabbing the note and flying toward the stairs.

"Come on, let's go! I'll read it on the way."

The surprised messenger hurried down the stairs in her wake, handed her up into the carriage and jumped up beside the driver. The carriage started forward with a jerk.

Ellie opened the note. Constance wrote that she'd had success and had instructed the driver to deliver Ellie to a particular address where she would meet her.

"Ellie!" She heard a shout behind the carriage. She peered through the window and looked back at the house. Robert stood at the bottom of the steps staring after the carriage. He waved his arms over his head to signal her. "Ellie, wait! Where are you going?" The carriage drove on, his shouts unheeded by all but the sobbing passenger inside.

****

Robert watched the carriage distance itself from him. He was certain Ellie had seen him. Where was she going? And in whose carriage? Why didn't she stop when he called?

If he'd had his druthers, he would have jumped into his own carriage to follow, but his grandmother and Melinda had taken it for the afternoon, leaving him stranded. He could certainly send someone to hire a private conveyance, but he would have no idea where Ellie had gone.

With a last look at the settling dust where the carriage had disappeared down the road, Robert turned back toward the stairs. He looked up at the house.

127

Perhaps Melinda's maid, Alice, would know where Ellie had gone. He took the stairs two at a time, hoping against hope that Stephen Sadler had not come by to pick her up for an outing. Would Ellie go with another man? An inexplicable sense of impending trouble drove him at full speed into the house.

His heart raced as he grabbed the banister and hauled himself up the stairs to the second floor.

"Alice?" he called. "Alice?"

The tiny redhead popped her head out of Melinda's room, several piles of clothing in her hand. Her eyes widened when she saw him. Suddenly winded, he bent double and struggled to catch his breath for a moment.

"Yes, Mr. Chamberlain? Are you all right?"

Robert nodded and swallowed hard. He straightened.

"Yes, yes. Thanks. Do you know where Miss Standish has gone, Alice?"

"Miss Standish, sir?" Alice stared at him.

"Yes, Alice, Miss Standish. She just left in a carriage. Did she say where she was going?"

Alice shook her wide-eyed head. "No, sir. I didn't know she had left the house."

Robert dropped his head and shook it, turning away with slumped shoulders. Perhaps she would return soon. He had no need to worry, either about her safety or her possible disappearance. He suspected that if the worst came to pass, if she indeed returned to her own time, it would occur as fast as her appearance...through whatever portal she had arrived. And he would know.

"Is there anything else, Mr. Chamberlain?"

"No, thank you, Alice," he called over his shoulder as he eyed Ellie's door. He moved slowly toward the door and laid a hand against it. It wasn't proper, but he simply could not resist. He wanted to smell her scent, to reassure himself that she had not vanished as suddenly as she came.

He pushed open the door and slid into the room. The bed was made, the room tidy. He crossed to the bed and ran his fingers across the pillow where her head had rested. He imagined her beautiful hair flowing across the pillow as she lay next to him. Would she lie next to him one day? Would his dreams come true?

Robert turned to leave the room and noticed several envelopes lying on the desk. His own name handwritten on the top envelope caught his attention, and he grabbed the white square and ripped it open. With a sinking heart, he read:

Dear Robert,

Thank you for everything you have given me over the last few days. I cannot tell you how grateful I am for your kind assistance on the train and the hospitality of your home.

I must go, Robert. I have made arrangements to stay elsewhere in the city, and I do not want you to try to find me. This is best for both of us. I cannot bear to hurt your feelings, and I am afraid I might if I stay with you any longer.

There is no graceful way to say this, so I will just blurt it out. I am engaged, Robert, to a man in Chicago, a man from my time. When I wake up from this wonderful dream, he will be there beside me, and I owe him my loyalty.

Please forgive me for running away like this. I could not look into your eyes and speak without stuttering.

Take care, Robert.

Ellie

Robert crushed the letter to his forehead and sagged onto the desk chair. He could not think straight. Pain seared through his chest. He could not breathe. Where had she gone? Why had she run from him? Engaged? Had he misread the sparkle in her eyes when she looked at him?

He lowered his fist and pressed open the letter once again, angry that he had crushed it. If the small white missive were all he had left of Ellie, he planned to treasure it. He straightened his shoulders and lifted his head. This was not over! He jumped up!

"Alice," he roared.

Alice came running down the hall and into the room. Her brown eyes threatened to pop out of her head.

"Mr. Chamberlain, what is it? What has happened?"

"Tell me everything you know about Miss Standish's activities today."

Chapter Twelve

After a tearful journey that seemed to last forever, the carriage delivered her to an older Victorian house in downtown Seattle. She stepped out to meet Constance, who waited on the steps of the house.

"Constance! I can't thank you enough for everything you've done."

"I am happy to help, Ellie, though your puffy face tells me that this decision has been difficult for you."

Ellie nodded but did not trust herself to talk.

"Come inside. Mrs. McGuire runs this rooming house. It is for ladies only. They will be sitting down to supper soon. Are you hungry?"

Ellie followed Constance up the wooden steps to a lovely, narrow, rose-colored, three-story house. Mrs. McGuire, a plump, gray-haired, motherly sort, met them at the door.

"Welcome, Miss Standish. It is a pleasure to have you. Please step into the parlor. May I offer you some tea? Dinner will be ready within the hour."

Constance answered for her. "Yes, please, let's have some tea, Mrs. McGuire. I think Miss Standish could use some refreshment." Ellie demurred, but Constance insisted.

Mrs. McGuire showed them into a comfortable room at the front of the house and left them alone while she fetched the tea. The soft rose and blue colors of the room served to soothe Ellie's jangled nerves. Lace curtains at the tall bay windows muted the light. Ellie sank onto the velvet rose sofa and took off her hat to ease the aching in her head. She closed her eyes and rubbed her temples.

"Does your head hurt?" Constance asked solicitously as she sat down beside Ellie on the couch.

Ellie opened her eyes and smiled wanly. "Yes."

"Some nice hot tea will do you a world of good."

At that moment, Mrs. McGuire returned with a silver

tea service and set it down on the cherrywood table in front of the sofa.

"I would love to sit and take tea with you ladies, but I must return to the kitchen, or I am likely to burn tonight's dinner." The plump woman beamed and left the room.

Constance poured some tea and gave Ellie a cup.

"You look very tired."

"I am. I hardly slept last night, and Robert arrived back at the house before I left."

"Yes?" Constance tilted her head inquiringly.

"I had left him a note. I wanted to leave before he came home. So, when the carriage came, I ran out the door." Ellie remembered her flight and giggled nervously, a sound that seemed inappropriate. She certainly didn't feel like laughing.

"You left without telling him? Why, Ellie?"

"I have my reasons, Constance. Please believe me. It was extremely difficult. Promise me you won't tell him where I am...although I suspect he won't want to know, after the ungrateful way I left the house."

"Oh, Ellie. I am so sorry."

Ellie looked at her former competition. "Just treat him well, Constance. I know you will."

Constance reddened and stood abruptly to walk to the window. "Ellie, I-I don't know what to say. The truth is...after today, I do not think I want to marry Robert anymore. I think he is quite taken with you, and I do not want a man who is in love with someone else."

At any other time, Ellie would have loved to hear those words, but she had burnt her bridges. There was no going back.

"I don't think he will fancy himself in love with me after he reads my letter, Constance. I told him I was engaged."

Constance turned from the window. She raised her eyebrows. "But I thought you said that was over. You are selling the ring."

"It is over...as far as I can tell. But that is what Robert needed to hear."

Constance approached and laid a gentle hand on her shoulder. "I cannot pretend to understand what is going

131

on here, Ellie, but I trust you know what you are doing."
She sighed. "Let's go up and see your room."

Constance led the way upstairs to the second floor,
where she opened a door on the right. The room was small
but cozy. A small twin bed with a bright yellow coverlet
rested against one wall. A highly polished mahogany
dresser with oval mirror, a well-varnished night table
with white glass lamp, and a small, rose velvet chair
completed the furnishings.

"The washroom is down the hall. Mrs. McGuire will
explain the house rules. I think they are standard. No
cooking in the rooms, no men beyond the parlor, no
overnight guests...that sort of thing."

Ellie shrugged. She knew she was in the Dark Ages,
and the light was only getting dimmer. When would she
wake up from this dream? It held no pleasure or
excitement for her any longer.

Constance wished her a good evening and said she
would pick her up the following day to take the ring to a
jeweler. Ellie fought the urge to beg her to stay, hating
how clingy and dependent she'd become. That she was
penniless and alone, without friends and family, a
hundred years before her time, did nothing to make her
feel better about her character flaws.

Though Ellie longed for nothing more than to curl up
into a ball on her bed and go to sleep, she dragged herself
downstairs at the sound of the dinner bell, thinking it
better to avoid creating undue interest and suspicion. She
longed for her credit card so she could book a cruise and
run away to the Caribbean. In fact, she wondered where
her purse was at the moment. Next to her bed in Chicago?
On a train to Seattle a hundred years from now? Clutched
in her lap while she rode the El and cried about the loss of
a fiancé?

Mrs. McGuire had set a lovely table, with white
linen, decorative porcelain dinnerware and a centerpiece
of bright yellow chrysanthemums. Three other women sat
at the table, all younger than Ellie. They wore
conventional clothing of white shirtwaist blouses and
tailored skirts. Their hairstyles were all similar, upswept
Gibsons in various designs depending on the shape and
texture of their hair.

They stared at Ellie in surprise for just a moment before smiling and welcoming her to the house. Mrs. McGuire made the introductions to Miss Samantha Stevens, Miss Martha Brown, and Miss Dorothy Simmons. Ellie shook hands with each of them and sat down in the indicated seat opposite Mrs. McGuire.

The young women were not much older than Melinda, and the conversation was lively. Ellie felt a sharp pang of regret. She would miss Melinda's bubbly personality. Samantha taught school, Martha worked as a typist at the newspaper, and Dorothy clerked in a bank. They asked Ellie questions about her stay in Seattle and her future plans, and Ellie fielded the answers as best she could. Certain her lies were growing more distorted with each embellishment and that she risked exposure, she hoped she would soon wake up or return to her own time...whichever the case might be. The latter still seemed farfetched. Wouldn't she know if she had traveled in time? Wouldn't she feel tired? Different? Older? Younger?

As depressed as she was, dinner proved to be a soothing gathering of women. The food was delicious, though Ellie had a frustrating moment when she had to explain once again that she didn't eat meat.

"Why not?" Dorothy asked, her fork in midair.

Ellie looked around the table at the sea of eyes that watched her curiously. The young women looked so similar in their white shirtwaist blouses and dark skirts. Only their hair color and body frames were different. Martha wore small round glasses on her pale face.

"I-I'm an animal lover, you see." Ellie gave a helpless shrug and bit into a delicious homemade biscuit, hoping they would take her answer at face value.

"Really?" Samantha, a petite blonde, murmured. "I love animals too, but..."

"What do you eat, then?" Dorothy asked with a napkin to her rosy face.

How could she tell them about the varied inventory of delicious vegetarian foods available in stores in the twenty-first century? She thought fast.

"Well, I eat a lot of vegetables, of course. I do eat cheese and eggs. Those are just like meat, really."

"Oh." Samantha nodded sagely. "Yes, I can see. There really must be quite a bit to eat besides meat."

"As you see, ladies, she has some potatoes and carrots on her plate, as well as having a glass of milk. She really has plenty to eat." Martha, future investigative reporter, pushed her glasses back up to the bridge of her nose.

"All right, girls, let's not badger Miss Standish any longer. Eat your dinner." Mrs. McGuire urged with a kindly look in Ellie's direction. "I'll prepare something additional for you tomorrow, Miss Standish."

"Oh, you don't have to go to any trouble for me, Mrs. McGuire. I choose not to eat meat. I don't expect anyone to put themselves out because of my choice. And please call me Ellie."

"May we all call you Ellie?" Samantha asked, with a scrunched-up button nose.

"Yes, please." Ellie felt like she was back in the classroom, calling on students who waved their hands in the air with questions.

"Wonderful," Dorothy murmured as she resumed eating.

While the girls continued their conversation regarding the day's events and the latest sighting of an attractive eligible bachelor, Ellie munched her food and listened with half an ear as she wondered what Robert was doing at the moment. She tried to imagine how he had handled her ungracious departure and wondered what he thought of her now. Hopefully, he would put her in the past as a temporary aberration in his world and move on...although Constance had indicated she might not be willing to consider him as a potential husband any longer.

Ellie bit her lip. She hoped she hadn't done any irreparable damage to Robert's life. Constance and he suited each other well, though it seemed likely that if Constance had not already fallen madly in love with him, she would not be doing so in the future. And perhaps mad, passionate love did not suit Robert. Ellie had seen Robert in the throes of infatuation. He'd become moody, aggressive, and unhappy—quite unlike the confident, witty, debonair man she'd met on the train. She hardly took his crush on her as a sign of true love, having never being one to incite such passion in men. She thought it more likely his fascination stemmed from his notion that she had traveled back in time. What man didn't like a good science fiction story...even at the turn of the century?

"Well, I am sure my boss will not say. He was absent from work for a few days and has been preoccupied since his return." Dorothy's words penetrated Ellie's distracted musings.

Ellie returned her focus to her current setting. The table for six was set with white linen and dishes of simple white porcelain. The dining room was much smaller than that in the Chamberlain home, but all the more cozy because of its reduced size. A well-polished mahogany china cabinet matched the sideboard, and both stood out impressively against pale blue walls. Sheer white lace curtains hung at the windows. Ellie studied as much detail as possible, hoping to store the memories away for when she returned to her own time...or woke up. This first-hand experience in the late Victorian/early Edwardian era could only help to inform her teachings.

Dinner ended on a festive note, and they all helped Mrs. McGuire clear the table and wash the dishes. When cleanup was done, Ellie professed herself exhausted after the long day and skipped the house's customary after-dinner tea in the parlor. She climbed the well-varnished wooden stairs to the second floor. After a brief stop in the washroom to wash her face and hands, Ellie returned to her room, shed her clothes, took down her hair and climbed into bed. She'd left any extra clothing belonging to Melinda at the house and would need to purchase a few things tomorrow, once she'd sold the ring...that is unless she finally woke up in her lonely apartment.

Ellie surveyed the room in the dark, noting how the moon came through the large window and cast silver beams across the walls. And she willed herself to sleep and to wake up from her Victorian dream. She'd had enough of the past. Her present didn't look very promising, if indeed Kyle had cancelled the wedding, but she didn't think life would hurt as much as it did here at the turn of the century.

****

135

Morning brought Constance in the carriage. Ellie climbed into the conveyance and off they went in a cloud of dust...literally.

"Ellie, I must say, you have created quite the maelstrom at the Chamberlain house."

Ellie caught her breath. Though Constance smiled, her eyes were quite serious.

"What do you mean?"

"When I arrived home last night, I had a message from Robert waiting for me. He wanted to know if I had assisted you in leaving, where you were, and if you were safe."

"Oh, Constance. I'm so sorry to have involved you. How did he know? Did you reply to the note?"

"I am not sure how he knew. Alice did meet me at the door when I came to visit you in the morning. Perhaps he questioned the servants." She paused and sighed. "At any rate, I did not have time to send a note around this morning before he appeared on my doorstep, only an hour ago, with the same questions." She smiled. "I would say he *demanded* the answers, but he is far too well bred to be so rude."

Ellie turned to stare out the window. The carriage rumbled along dirt roads as they passed a bevy of lovely Victorian homes which appeared startlingly...new.

"I don't know what to say." Shame kept her from meeting Constance's eyes.

"Well, Ellie, I think one thing is for certain. You made quite an impression on Robert, one he is not likely to forget as soon as you think. I knew that from the first moment he introduced you on the train."

Ellie turned startled eyes to Constance. "I-I hoped he would accept my thanks, take the engagement at face value, and let me go."

Constance gave her head a slight shake and grimaced. "He might still. I assured him that you were safe, but I refused to tell him where you were. He asked me about your plans to be married, and I confirmed that I knew you had been engaged. While I did not lie to him directly, I think he believes the engagement is ongoing." Constance bit her lip and looked at Ellie. "He seems to be very infatuated with you, Ellie. He has never looked at me like that once. Are you sure you are doing the right thing?"

Ellie sighed and brushed away an escaping tear with the back of her hand. "No, Constance, I am not sure about anything, except that my time here is limited, and I cannot stay. I thought I should leave before we fell in love...well, before I fell in love, I should say."

"It may be too late. He is already in love, Ellie."

Ellie turned stricken eyes on Constance.

"Oh, Constance, surely not! It has only been a few days! If he is infatuated, I think it is only a fascination with someone from...uh...another place, from Chicago."

Constance burst out into a surprisingly rich, husky laugh. "Chicago?" she chortled. "Robert is well traveled. He has been to Chicago many times! No, I do not think that is it. I think it is probably you. You are quite unique, Ellie."

"Not in my own world," Ellie muttered with a red face. Her theory did sound silly without being able to explain "Chicago" meant a hundred years into the future.

"Pardon?"

"Nothing. I was just thinking aloud." She patted Constance's hand. "Thank you for not telling him where I was. Hopefully, he'll just assume I'm engaged and move on."

"Perhaps," Constance murmured. The carriage came to a halt in front of a jeweler's shop, and Ellie followed Constance into the elegant establishment. Constance, an unexpected fairy godmother in disguise, expertly negotiated a hefty sum for the ring, and they sailed out of the store with enough money to buy Ellie a few clothes, some necessities, and room and board for at least a year, should she need. Ellie convinced Constance that her luggage had been lost on the train, and it was under this assumption that Constance took her to a series of ready-to-wear stores to buy some tailored suits, dresses and undergarments.

With bags and hatboxes in hand, they hopped aboard the carriage once again and stopped to refresh themselves and rest in a teashop in downtown Seattle. Ellie followed Constance into the small shop on the first floor of a three-story brick building on a busy main street. Ellie had lost her bearings and had no earthly idea where she was in the city. The streets looked completely different with hard-packed dirt instead of asphalt. Street signs seemed to be in short supply, and the absence of traffic lights stumped her. Without the view from the elevated interstate which passed through the modern city, without the Space Needle or the gleaming skyscrapers with their glass windows, Ellie couldn't even figure out where she was in relation to the waterfront of Elliott Bay. Her world had suddenly become much smaller, consisting of a few dirt roads, forests of pine trees, a neighborhood of similar Victorian houses and the shopping and business district in which they currently drank tea.

A young African-American waiter in white coat and black slacks seated them at a small round table, took their order and left. Ellie ordered the same items as Constance, tea and a scone, neither of which she particularly craved but both sounding like something a turn-of-the-century woman might order.

"Where are we, Constance? I can't seem to get my bearings." Ellie adjusted her hat, wondering if she would ever learn to ignore it as some of her fellow female tea drinkers did.

"We're on Second Avenue. I thought you had not been to Seattle before, Ellie." Constance eyed Ellie inquisitively as she laid her napkin across her lap.

Ellie colored. "No, I haven't. I was just wondering where we were in relation to the rest of the city, to the bay, that's all."

"Ah." Constance nodded in understanding. "I do not really know, to tell you the truth. I leave that up to my driver."

Tea arrived in a plain porcelain teapot with matching white cups, along with scones on a simple white plate. Constance poured.

"I was surprised to find so much ready-to-wear clothing in the store. I thought..." *Careful, Ellie.* "I thought...we might have to visit a dressmaker."

Constance took a sip of tea and smiled. "This *is* the twentieth century, Ellie. We have a great many more modern conveniences than we did a decade ago. When I think back on the fashions back then! Parting our hair in the middle? Those uncomfortable bustles and large crinolines? Do you remember? I am so grateful those days are gone. I love these sleek, modern styles." She ran a hand down the sleeve of her emerald green tailored silk jacket, the picture of elegance.

Ellie's eyes crinkled, and she wanted to burst out laughing, but she pressed her lips together. To Constance, this clothing *was* the height of fashion, and Ellie had to admit it was much more stylish than her bulky turtleneck sweater, denim skirt and clogs, now safely stowed away in her dresser at the rooming house.

Ellie murmured her assent. She gazed out the window at the busy street. Carriages and wagons passed to and fro, kicking up dust in their wake.

"Oh, dear," Constance murmured almost under her breath. She stiffened and stared out the window.

Ellie followed her eyes. "What is it?"

"Oh, dear. I had hoped. Well, this was the only teashop near the stores. I-I hoped..."

"What, Constance? Is something wrong?"

Constance turned to Ellie, a disconcerted look in her eyes. Her apologetic smile put Ellie on the edge of her seat.

Constance nodded in the direction of the window. "I did not tell you before, because I thought he would not...that is I did not know he was at work today." She looked back at the window. "That is Robert's bank across the street, and his carriage has just arrived."

Ellie's eyes darted to the window and she froze, her heart thumping in her throat. Robert descended from the carriage and strode rapidly inside a large brick building with the name "Washington Bank" over the door. From this distance, she could see nothing more than that he was dressed well...as always, and that his stride seemed purposeful and determined...as always. However, the sight of him renewed the ache in her heart. Such a handsome man! But a much more vulnerable man than she had previously thought. Underneath that confident exterior lurked a man who longed for love, and he deserved a real live woman...not a figment of his imagination...or hers.

"Can we go, Constance? I'm afraid he'll reach his

office and see us leaving from a window."

"Yes, certainly, of course. I am very sorry about this, Ellie. I should have had the driver find another shop." She rose from the table.

Ellie rose on shaking knees and held onto the back of her chair. "No, no, that's not your fault. But to see him so soon..." She wondered if her face was as pale as it felt. "I had hoped to be settled before I saw him next...if ever."

Constance moved toward the door, and Ellie followed her outside. Ellie could have died to see that their carriage was down the road about a block. She felt exposed and vulnerable to the three-story building with seemingly hundreds of windows across the street, and she turned her back to the street to hide her face. She heard the clop of the horses' hooves nearing, though the carriage's progress seemed unbearably slow.

"The carriage is here, Ellie. Get in." Ellie turned and climbed in, and Constance followed. The carriage started forward, and with a sigh of relief, Ellie peeked out to study the building where Robert worked. She gasped when she saw Robert standing on the sidewalk staring after their carriage, and she ducked her head back in to press back into the corner of her seat.

"He saw us, Constance. Oh, I can't believe I had to stick my head out the window." Ellie felt perfectly awful, her eyes threatened to release a torrent of tears.

"Are you sure? Ellie, I cannot tell you how sorry I am. What a silly decision on my part."

"Yes, I'm sure he saw. He was standing in front of the bank watching the carriage."

Constance peered out the window.

"I do not see him, Ellie."

Ellie took another chance and stuck her head out the window again to look behind. Robert no longer stood on the sidewalk, but his carriage was in motion, and it moved in their direction!

Chapter Thirteen

Ellie pulled her head back in, banging her hat on the edge of the door. With wild eyes, she turned to Constance. "He's right behind us! I-I think he's following us. Can the driver speed up?" Visions of old western movies with masked desperados chasing racing stagecoaches as they careened wildly out of control popped into her mind.

Constance stared at Ellie with round eyes and shook her head slowly.

"Speed up? Do you mean go faster?"

Ellie gave her a fervent nod.

"We cannot go faster, Ellie. This is a city street. Robert is a gentleman. He would not follow us to the boarding house. That would be quite irregular for a man of his upbringing and stature."

Ellie eyed her skeptically, remembering the only boyfriend she'd had in her teen years...a romance lasting one whole week, and how she'd followed him one night to another girl's house. Had things really changed that much in a hundred years?

"Are you sure, Constance?"

Constance nodded firmly. "Yes. If Robert really wants to talk to you, I am sure he will contact me, and I will let you know. Remember, he thinks you are engaged. I do not see Robert as the sort of man who would interfere with such a promise."

It was all Ellie could do not to peek outside the carriage again, but she resisted the compelling urge. Not to mention her head hurt where her hatpin must have pulled out hair when she'd smacked her hat on the carriage window.

The ride back to the rooming house seemed to take forever, and in between bouts of overwhelming anxiety, Ellie tried to understand the origin of her fear. Was she afraid to face Robert, to reaffirm that she was indeed engaged and not available? Lies, all lies. Was she afraid that with one look into his emerald green eyes she would fly into his arms and beg him to take her back? True story. Was she afraid that he just wanted to have one last conversation with her, to tell her he despised her? All of the above were correct.

At long last, the carriage pulled up to the sweetly painted Victorian house fronted by rose bushes in riotous bloom, and Constance stepped out. Ellie kept her head inside but peeked through the window. She saw no other conveyances on the quiet, tree-lined street.

"Well, of all the nerve!" Constance muttered as she stared down the street.

"What?" Ellie froze, bent over awkwardly as she prepared to descend from the carriage.

"Wait right there. I am going to have a word with him."

Ellie swallowed hard. Was it Robert? Her back began to hurt from the unnatural posture. Should she sit down or get out of the carriage? She couldn't stand in her current ridiculous position any longer.

She cautiously stepped down and saw Robert's carriage pulled up near some neighboring houses. He wasn't visible, but Constance stood at the foot of his carriage seemingly in a heated discussion as she pointed to her own carriage and vehemently shook her head.

Unsure of what to do, Ellie threw one look at Robert's driver, who watched Constance curiously, and then made a mad dash for the front door of the house. She closed the heavy teak door behind her and turned to peer out of the lovely leaded glass. Robert had now descended from his carriage, and he pointed to the house.

"Ellie! How was your day?"

Ellie whirled around to see Mrs. McGuire emerging from the kitchen, wiping her hands on a white apron.

"Oh, wonderful. We managed to do a lot of shopping." She twisted around to look out the door once again.

"Where are your bags? Are they out in the carriage? May I help you carry them in?"

"No!" Ellie almost shrieked. She blushed at the startled look on Mrs. McGuire's face. "No, thank you. Mrs. Green will help me with them. She is just talking to someone right now."

Mrs. McGuire moved to the door to peer out. "Oh, I see. Is that...? Is that Mr. Robert Chamberlain? Why, yes, it is! How wonderful! I think I will just go and say hello."

Before Ellie knew what was happening, Mrs. McGuire had pulled open the door and stepped onto the porch to wave at Robert. Ellie slumped against the nearest wall. Had the world suddenly gone mad? How could Mrs. McGuire possibly know Robert?

She peered out again to see Mrs. McGuire approach the carriage. Robert and Constance turned, and then Robert shook Mrs. McGuire's hand with his ready smile and a slight dip of his handsome head. Even from this distance Ellie could see that Mrs. McGuire was under his thrall. Wasn't everybody? Ellie fumed.

In unison, all three turned toward the house. Ellie panicked. Robert was going to come in. What should she do? She eyed the staircase, wondering if she could drag her skirts up to the second floor in time to avoid a meeting. Without further thought, she grabbed a handful of material, bunched it up around her knees and took two steps.

"Ellie...Miss Standish. Mr. Chamberlain and Mrs. Green are staying to tea. Won't you join us?"

Ellie dropped her skirts and turned around on the stairs. She grasped the banister with a cold, clammy palm. Mrs. McGuire beamed, Constance eyed her with a mixture of apprehension and apology, and Robert watched her with a small enigmatic smile.

"Well, I was just about to—"

"Yes, Miss Standish, please join us. You might not know, Mrs. McGuire, but Miss Standish is already a friend of my family." He turned on the charm and flashed his captivating boyish dimples at Mrs. McGuire.

The older woman turned to Robert with rosy cheeks. "No, I did not know that. Though why would I? Ellie, Mr. Chamberlain is my banker. He helped me keep my house when my husband died. Please come down to tea."

Ellie could do nothing but return to the ground floor. Mrs. McGuire showed them to the parlor, with promises to return momentarily with refreshment.

Robert paused at the door and allowed Constance and Ellie to enter ahead of him. Constance seated herself on the lovely rose sofa. Ellie dropped down beside her, keeping her eyes on the dark blue and old rose oriental carpet, though she watched Robert in her peripheral vision. He walked over to the window and gazed out onto the street with his hands clasped behind his back. Ellie threw Constance a quick inquiring look, but Constance gave her head a small shake and an almost imperceptible shrug of her elegant shoulders.

Robert returned to stand by the fireplace. Out of the corner of her eye, Ellie watched him lean one arm on the mantle and stare down into the empty hearth. She fixed her eyes back on the carpeting, willing Mrs. McGuire to return as soon as possible.

"Well, ladies, I find myself at a loss for words." A small mirthless chuckle followed Robert's words.

Ellie's eyes flew to his face. His eyes were those of a stranger, his smile polished but flat. He looked at Ellie without expression and then to Constance.

Ellie slid her eyes to Constance who stared at Robert with narrowed eyes and pink spots on her cheeks.

"Now, see here, Robert—" Constance began.

The door opened, and Mrs. McGuire entered with the tea service. Robert sprang forward to close the door behind her.

"Well, here we are. Isn't this cozy?" the effervescent little woman asked as she set the tray down on the small coffee table in front of the sofa.

Ellie didn't particularly think so, and Constance looked like she wished herself elsewhere. Robert's face reanimated at Mrs. McGuire's arrival.

She poured four cups of tea, handed them out with sugars or cream as her guests desired and seated herself in a high-backed, dark blue velvet chair. Robert took the seat beside her and across from the sofa. Ellie kept her eyes on her tea, seemingly intent on divining her future in the bottom of the cup.

"Well!" the happy hostess murmured. "Seattle is such a small world. Who could suspect we would all know each other?"

Ellie's eyes flew to Robert, though he beamed at Mrs. McGuire. Who knew, indeed?

"I must say, Mrs. McGuire, that it was with some

surprise that I found both Mrs. Green and Miss Standish here today. I just happened along the street and saw them descending from the carriage in front of your lovely home...and now here I am, having tea with a bevy of beautiful women. How fortunate can one man be?"

Mrs. McGuire tittered and blushed, while Ellie dropped her jaw at Robert's blatant lie and flirtatious lines. She slid a look toward Constance, whose lips twitched as she watched Robert.

"Oh, for goodness' sake, Mr. Chamberlain, I am sure you must not include me in your bevy." Mrs. McGuire delicately raised a small linen napkin to her face.

"Oh, but I do, Mrs. McGuire."

Ellie gulped her tea and relaxed into her seat to watch Robert at his finest. Perhaps the two of them would chat the entire time, and she could escape without a word.

"Ellie, how do you come to know Mr. Chamberlain and his family? Do you bank with him?"

Her eyes flew to Robert who turned to watch her with the same half smile she could not interpret. "Um...I...uh...met them on the train."

"Oh, really! How nice!" Mrs. McGuire took a sip of tea. "I must tell you that when Mr. McGuire passed on, he left me in quite a pickle with the house. It was not paid for, and he left little insurance, so Mr. Chamberlain suggested I turn the house into a boarding establishment. He made all the arrangements for the bank to accept payments from the profits of the house. I consider him a most trusted financial advisor...and a dear friend." She beamed and reached over to pat his hand as it rested on his knee.

Robert had the grace to blush.

"It was my pleasure, Mrs. McGuire. I must say you are doing a remarkable job."

"Thank you." She eyed him with a twist of her lips. "Although I should note that this is the first time Mr. Chamberlain has had time to accept my invitation to tea. He works very hard and has little time for socializing."

Robert cast a quick, enigmatic glance at Ellie before he looked away to take a sip of tea.

"Yes, that is true, Mrs. McGuire. In all the years I have known Robert, I do not think he has taken more than an hour or two at lunch. Now, I have seen him on several outings over the last few days. How nice of you to join us today, Robert." Constance chimed in with an amused note in her voice.

"Well, as I mentioned, I was in the neighborhood and...ah—"

"Yes, you did mention that. And what brings you to this neighborhood, Mr. Chamberlain?" Ellie surprised herself most of all when she spoke. She hoped to tease him as Constance had, to watch the adorable color on his grave face.

Robert's eyes narrowed and he turned his head in her direction, staring hard at her. "Well, the truth is, Miss Standish, I thought I saw an old friend of mine with whom I had a misunderstanding. I heard that he became engaged recently, and I wanted to congratulate him and tell him we must let bygones be bygones." High color stained his cheeks and he tightened his lips. "But alas, I could not catch up to him. Now, perhaps I will never get a chance to talk to him again."

Tears sprang to Ellie's eyes, and she ran a hand over her face as if she had a headache. From the side, she saw Constance throw a mortified glance her way.

"I miss my friend," Robert added in a quiet note.

"Oh, my dear Mr. Chamberlain, what a sad story. Is there no hope of reconciliation? Do you know where he lives? Can you drop him a note?"

Robert shook his head. "No, Mrs. McGuire, I do not know where he lives. I am afraid there is no hope of reconciliation. It seems he is lost to me forever."

Ellie couldn't hold back a sob, and she jumped up. "Excuse me. I have such a headache." She stumbled toward the exit, but Robert jumped up to open the door for her. He turned his back to the room and brushed tender fingers against the side of her face as she passed.

"Ellie."

She heard him whisper her name, but she turned away as she grabbed her skirts and flew up the stairs to her room. Heedless of the pain, she dragged off her hat, threw herself on the bed and buried her face in her pillow, sobbing and sobbing like she had never cried before.

Within ten minutes, a small tap on the door heralded

the arrival of Constance. She came in at Ellie's response and sat down on the edge of the bed. Ellie wiped her face on the back of her sleeve and turned on her side, pulling her knees up in a modified fetal position.

"Ellie, do you really have a headache? I am so sorry you feel poorly."

Ellie nodded, wishing for nothing more than the over-the-counter pain reliever sitting in her medicine cabinet at home.

Constance peered sympathetically at Ellie's face. "You have been crying. Robert's story was quite a ploy to make you feel bad, was it not?"

Ellie rubbed her head against the pillow and nodded. "I guess I deserve it. I should have had the courage to tell him in person that I was leaving...but I wasn't sure if I could leave once I saw him."

"I understand," Constance murmured. "Robert and the driver brought in your bags. They are downstairs."

"Is he gone?" Ellie sniffed.

Constance nodded. "Yes. He made his excuses as soon as you left."

"Mrs. McGuire really loves him, doesn't she?"

"Many people do. He is known to be a very generous and kind man."

Ellie pushed herself up into a sitting position. She held her pillow to her chest and rested her face against it.

"Why hasn't he married before now, Constance?"

Constance blushed. "I do not know. You know, of course, that I hoped he would ask me...after my husband died. But that did not happen...and I know now it never will."

Ellie nuzzled the edge of her pillow.

"He told me that he hadn't found a woman who could put up with him yet, and then he said he had never fallen in love." She looked at Constance. "How is it possible to be almost forty and never have fallen in love?" At her words, she saw Kyle's face. Had she ever really been in love with him?

Constance stared out the window above Ellie's bed. "I do not know. I fell in love at eighteen with the most wonderful young man...my husband." She sighed. "Robert works a great deal. He has always worked hard to support his family. His parents died when Melinda was young, and he took over parental duties. I do not think he ever had many opportunities to gad about town as a young bachelor might."

"But the train trip. He seemed so relaxed. And all those young women?"

Constance scoffed. "Girls! I know for certain that Robert is not interested in young girls. Those are Melinda's friends, and while his grandmother would prefer he choose someone that young for...em...the purposes of bearing a large, healthy family, he is not attracted to young, simpering girls."

"Are you certain you and he...?" It galled Ellie to ask, but if she had to give him up to someone, she preferred it be Constance.

Constance flushed and shook her head. "No, I am certain. At any rate, I have met someone."

Ellie dropped her pillow. "Who?" she asked with wide eyes.

"A certain Mr. Malcolm Stidwell. Perhaps you met him...at the dinner party the other night?" Constance took on a girlish coyness that brought a sparkle to her dark eyes.

Ellie grinned. "The handsome man with the silver hair."

"Yes. Silver hair."

Ellie leaned forward to give Constance an unexpected hug. "Oh, good for you, Constance!"

"Well, we will see. I do not know how we will get along, but I am to go to the park with him tomorrow."

"Fabulous!" Ellie leaned back and surveyed Constance, whose cheeks burned bright.

"As you say, fabulous!" Constance eyed Ellie thoughtfully. "Ellie, you should come with us. Please say you will."

"Oh, Constance, I can't. I mean...it's your first date. How would that look? You don't want me there."

Constance laughed. "Oh, yes, I do. First date, indeed! I would much prefer it if I had a female companion there. Please come. You cannot stay cooped up in this house all day."

"Are you sure, Constance?" Ellie wrinkled her nose

uncertainly.

Constance gave her a firm nod. "Yes, I am sure. I would be grateful if you could...em...facilitate my first...date as you say...with Malcolm. I fear I shall be too tongue-tied to say a word."

"All right, then. I owe you a lot. I'll come."

"Wonderful!" Constance rose and turned toward the door. "We will pick you up tomorrow at noon."

"Tomorrow," Ellie echoed as she watched Constance leave the room. She closed her eyes and willed herself to sleep, but its merciful oblivion eluded her.

Mrs. McGuire popped her head in shortly to see how Ellie fared and to inquire about her desires for dinner. Feeling extremely guilty about running out on the hospitable woman's tea party as she had, Ellie agreed to come down to dinner.

Dinner with the girls was a panacea for any depressed woman. Their lively chatter, occasional bickering and genuine friendship left no room for miserable faces at the table. Mrs. McGuire ran the boarding house much like her personality—bubbly, energetic, full of warmth and love.

"Dorothy, did you know that Mr. Chamberlain was here today?" Mrs. McGuire grinned and cast a sly glance in Ellie's direction.

Dorothy's eyes widened. "Oh, my goodness, really?" She drew her brows together for a quick moment. "Did I do something wrong?"

Ellie watched the exchange with confusion. What were they talking about? Did Dorothy know the man, too? Was there one woman on the planet who had not yet met the aggravating man?

"No, dear, he did not say anything about you. He said he was in the neighborhood and came for tea. Miss Standish...Ellie knows him, as well." Mrs. McGuire nodded in Ellie's direction. "This is such a small world!"

Ellie held her fork in midair. What?

All three girls turned curious eyes on Ellie. Dorothy cocked her head in inquiry.

"Do you know Mr. Chamberlain, Ellie?"

Ellie stuffed food in her mouth and nodded...now unable to discuss the matter since her mouth was full.

"Oh." Dorothy turned an inquiring look on Mrs. McGuire.

"She met him on the train to Seattle." Mrs. McGuire happily supplied the details.

"Really?" Dorothy continued to eye Ellie with a curious stare.

Ellie nodded and attacked her plate for another large mouthful of food.

"That would be when he took his sister and her friends to Spokane for her birthday."

Ellie looked up in surprise.

"Mr. Chamberlain is my employer. He is the head of the bank where I work. Mrs. McGuire recommended me to him, and he hired me as a clerk."

Ellie's cheeks burned, and she chewed her food with a nod.

"Well, perhaps you know, then, Ellie. He has hardly been at the bank lately, and people are wondering where he has been." Dorothy bit her lip. "I mean he is *always* at the bank. Every single day. The first person in to work and the last to leave. But for the last few days, he has only been in the bank for a few hours. Today, he dashed out of the bank as soon as he got there, and he never returned."

Ellie froze and threw a glance at Mrs. McGuire.

"Well, that is very interesting, Dorothy. Of course, you know he stopped by here for tea, but he said he was just in the neighborhood looking for an old friend."

"Do not misunderstand. I do not wish to gossip, but some people in the bank are talking." Dorothy pressed the issue, and Ellie's face burned.

"Dorothy, dear, are you sure this is not Mr. Chamberlain's private life and best not discussed at the dinner table?" Mrs. McGuire regarded her with a kind smile but her eyes brooked no argument.

"Yes, Mrs. McGuire." Dorothy smiled and returned to her food.

"Oh, please tell us what they have been saying at the bank, Dorothy. Now, you have us all agog to hear." Samantha piped up, seconded by Martha.

Dorothy glanced at Mrs. McGuire, who looked as if she, too, couldn't wait to hear the story.

Ellie wondered if she could just crawl under the table and die...but first, she had to hear the gossip.

"Well," Mrs. McGuire drew the word out, "if it is nothing disrespectful, I might like to hear."

"Oh no! It is rather curious, in fact. The other clerks say that he has fallen in love!" Dorothy delivered the sentence as if she'd dropped a bomb and waited for the fallout.

Samantha and Martha stared for a moment, then resumed eating, the matter of Mr. Chamberlain's love life obviously not of great importance. Ellie swallowed hard, a dry piece of bread lodged in her throat threatening to choke her. She grabbed for her glass of water and gulped. Mrs. McGuire threw her a quick glance.

"Really?" the older woman murmured. "How do they know such a personal detail?"

Dorothy warmed to her audience. "Well, another clerk's mother said they saw him at the park the other day with a woman...and that he appeared quite infatuated with her. I have never heard of Mr. Chamberlain doing anything so frivolous as to stroll about the park in the middle of the day. I think that is very significant." Dorothy quirked an eyebrow.

Ellie didn't miss Mrs. McGuire's quick glance in her direction, but she smiled and resumed eating, though she felt slightly nauseous.

"That does sound promising. Well, if he has finally met someone, I am happy for him. I began to think he was a confirmed bachelor." With a last lingering look at Ellie, Mrs. McGuire returned to her food.

"We all did," Dorothy murmured. "I hoped he was waiting for me." She grinned unexpectedly and dug into her food with bright pink cheeks.

"Oh, he is too old for you, silly!" Samantha and Martha giggled and poked her teasingly in the ribs, and Dorothy snickered along with them. Ellie knew how the young girl felt. Robert was hard to resist. She averted her eyes from Mrs. McGuire, who'd already given her several curious looks during the conversation.

****

The following day, Ellie dressed in her new clothing, a white shirtwaist with a soft lace collar and a

conservative, tailored suit in dark chocolate brown. She
surveyed herself in the small oval mirror. The color
flattered her brown eyes. She loved the lace at the sleeves
and the way the skirt fell away from her hips to the floor.
The fitted jacket trailed down to her knees like a brown
tuxedo, and she wondered how comfortable it would be
when she had to sit down. She'd done her hair as best she
could in an upswept Gibson and perched a matching
brown velvet hat with harvest gold ribbons on her head.
She twirled and preened in front of the mirror, very
satisfied with her first Victorian era purchase.

Ellie went downstairs and told Mrs. McGuire she was
going to the park with Constance for the afternoon. Mrs.
McGuire looked up distractedly from the stove, smiled
and wished her an enjoyable outing. A carriage pulled up
outside at noon, and Constance and Malcolm Stidwell
presented themselves at the door. On closer inspection,
she saw that the silver-haired gentleman had eyes of a
peaceful sky blue and his smile held a note of gentle
humor.

"Miss Standish, it is very nice to meet you at last. I
am afraid we were not introduced the other night at the
dinner party."

Ellie stuck out her hand. He blinked and took it in
his own. "Mr. Stidwell, thank you for taking me along on
your outing. I hope I'm not in the way."

"Not at all, Miss Standish. We are happy to have you
along, isn't that so, Constance?"

"Yes, Malcolm. I was very pleased when Ellie
accepted my invitation."

"Shall we, ladies?" Malcolm indicated the waiting
carriage. Ellie climbed in first, followed by Constance and
then Malcolm, who sat on the opposite seat. He kept up a
pleasant running commentary on the city as they made
their way to the park. The carriage dropped them off in
the same location as before, when she'd come with Robert,
and she tried to block the memory from her mind.
Unsuccessful, she settled for blocking Robert from her
mind...just for the day.

Malcolm held out both arms, and Constance took one
while Ellie reluctantly took the other. They promenaded
along the boardwalk by the lake, and Ellie kept silent

while the other two chatted. She allowed the tall Malcolm to guide them as she strolled mechanically, lost in memories of handsome dimples and dark-lashed green eyes.

"Isn't that right, Ellie?" Constance's voice broke through.

Ellie returned to the present. "I'm sorry. What?"

Malcolm laughed. "She has been daydreaming, I see. A penny for your thoughts, Ellie."

She tossed him a quick grin. "Oh, that's way too much money for one of my scatterbrained thoughts."

"Malcolm, Constance, Miss Standish. How do you do? May I join you for a moment?"

"Robert! How nice to see you out of the bank! What brings you out on such a fine day?" Malcolm nodded jovially.

Robert eyed a stunned Ellie for a moment. "The same as you, I expect, Malcolm. Warm sunshine and pleasant company."

Malcolm laughed. "Well, as you can see, I have my hands full with pleasant company. Ellie, would you care to walk with Robert?"

Chapter Fourteen

Ellie gritted her teeth and smiled up at the innocent Malcolm. Other than causing a scene, she had little choice except to release Malcolm's arm and take the one that Robert proffered. They fell into step behind Malcolm and Constance, who threw a quick glance over her shoulder to meet Ellie's stricken eyes.

Ellie attempted to stay close to Malcolm and Constance, thereby avoiding an intimate conversation, but Robert thwarted those plans by lagging a few steps behind them. With her hand tucked in his arm, there was little she could do.

"It is nice to see you, Ellie."

Ellie locked her eyes on Malcolm's back. "Thank you, Robert. It is nice to see you," she replied mechanically.

"How is your head today?"

She blinked and looked up at him. His eyes almost caught hers in a lock, but she dropped her gaze quickly. "My head? Oh, yes, my headache. That's fine, thank you."

"I am glad."

"How do you come to be here, Robert?"

"Oh, I stopped by the boarding house...to see Mrs. McGuire...and she informed me that you and Constance had come to the park with a man," he replied airily. "I thought it a fine day for an outing myself. I was pleased to see that Malcolm was taking good care of you two."

Ellie tipped her head to raise a skeptical eye in his direction, but she remained mute.

He dropped the airy note, and his voice grew husky. "I must say I was surprised to read of your engagement. I wonder that you did not share the news with me when we first met."

Ellie faltered for a moment. Robert steadied her and she recovered.

"I-I...it didn't come up. It didn't seem important at the time." She avoided eye contact.

Robert gave a short mirthless laugh. "Not important? How is that possible?"

"When should I have told you, Robert? The moment I met you? When I realized I was lost on a hundred-year-old train with no money and no phone? When you took me into your home? When..." She couldn't say anymore.

"When I kissed you...and you returned the kiss?" Robert squeezed her hand against his arm. Her heart rolled over. Against her will, she welcomed the warmth of his body. "That would have been an opportune moment to tell me, Ellie."

"I know. I'm sorry, Robert. You're right." She peeked up at him to see that now it was he who stared straight ahead.

"Tell me about this...fiancé of yours. He is from your time, is he not? You have not gone and engaged yourself to Mr. Sadler already, have you?"

"Robert!" She almost chuckled. She didn't want to talk about Kyle. He seemed like a lifetime ago...unless she woke up with him next to her in bed tomorrow morning. "I don't want to talk about him. He doesn't seem to belong to this time," she murmured, forgetting who she was talking to for a moment.

Robert paused and turned her to face him. "You are right, Ellie. He does not belong to this time. He belongs to a past life. You are here now...in my time...with me."

She stared at the disarming cleft in his chin, unwilling to meet his eyes, to drown in them and throw herself into his arms. She needed to stay strong.

"Robert, it's time we woke up...both of us. There is no past life, no other time. This is just a dream, and a very bittersweet one at that." She finally met his eyes and fought against the love he allowed her to see. "What if we wake up tomorrow, and I am home alone in my bed, and you are here alone in yours? Then what? What is the point of falling in love in a dream? To wake to a painful, lonely reality?" Her voice cracked, and she was only vaguely aware that Malcolm and Constance had paused to look back at them but had moved on again.

Robert grabbed her hands in his, uncaring of who saw.

"I love you, Ellie. I do not care if it is a dream or

whether you have come to me from the future. I love you, and leaving me is not going to change that."

Ellie longed for nothing more than to move into his embrace and bury herself against his chest. In a perfect dream, she could have done just that. Why couldn't she just throw caution to the winds and give in? She couldn't remember her reasons for leaving. What were they? They had seemed valid and necessary at the time.

She pulled her hands from his and walked on. He caught up to her and tucked her hand under his arm once again.

She glanced up at him, grief forcing a confession from her. "I miss you, Robert. You are the only person who truly knows me here, the only one who knows where I come from."

"All the more reason to return to me, Ellie." His voice was husky.

"If I knew why I was here...if I knew that I wouldn't suddenly wake up one morning in my time...and be unable to recapture the dream to get back to you. If I knew for certain that I had traveled in time and would not return..." She stopped and turned to him. "What makes you think I won't simply disappear? Do you want to risk that?"

Robert nodded grimly. "I would risk anything for you, Ellie, for the way I feel when I am with you." He gave her an ironic smile. "And perhaps you have forgotten. You did *simply disappear*...from my home."

She grimaced and shook her head. "You're infatuated with a creature of your imagination, a character from a science fiction novel who travels back in time." She dropped her head. "That's not me. I'm just a regular woman who has hardly ever incited a great passion in any man. In fact, I never have." She looked up at him with a rueful smile.

"Miss Standish, Robert! How do you do?" Ellie turned a startled face toward Stephen Sadler. She smiled weakly and cast a quick glance at Robert hoping he would behave. He gave Stephen a brief nod, but Ellie saw a flash in his narrowed eyes.

"Sadler, how do you do?"

"I am well, thank you, Robert. It is a fine day at the

park, isn't it? How have you been, Ellie?" Ellie saw the blue of his eyes harden for a moment in response to Robert's curt greeting.

"Fine, thank you, Stephen." Ellie stood between the two men who exchanged unspoken words, and she wondered if there was a shortage of women in Seattle at the moment. Or was her dream prepared to indulge her in every possible fantasy, including the jealousy of two very handsome Victorian men?

"Ah, there you are, Ellie! We are about to have a late lunch. Good day, Stephen. Won't you join us, gentlemen?" The irrepressible Malcolm arrived, with Constance in tow, to make matters worse.

"Certainly, I would love to," Stephen murmured.

"My pleasure," Robert responded, taking up Ellie's hand once again. Constance cast her a sympathetic look, but Ellie was sure that the other woman's lips twitched ever so slightly.

The group sashayed off the boardwalk and toward the picnic area. Malcolm's driver had laid out a sumptuous feast on a linen-covered table, much as Robert had supplied two days ago. Ellie found herself seated between Robert and Stephen and across from a twinkling Malcolm and apologetic Constance.

Malcolm served food while Constance, Robert and Stephen chatted about innocuous matters such as the weather. Ellie kept her lips sealed as she surveyed the faces of the people at her table. Was it possible that she actually sat in the company of three men and a woman from the turn of the century? In her time, they would all be dead long ago. She shuddered for a moment. The thought was too horrible to contemplate.

"Ellie, would you like my jacket? You look cold." Robert spoke low near her ear.

"Oh, I'm fine," she murmured.

Stephen beat him to it by whipping off his outer coat and settling it on her shoulders.

"There you are, Ellie."

"Oh, thank you. Thank you very much."

Ellie stared hard at Constance who watched the exchange of glances between the men with wide eyes and a lift at the corner of her mouth.

"You were telling me about your engagement a few moments ago, Ellie. When is the happy day?" Ellie turned a startled eye to Robert who threw Stephen a challenging glance over Ellie's head. She shot Constance a harried glance. Malcolm raised his eyebrows.

"Many felicitations, Ellie," Malcolm murmured.

"Ellie. I did not know. Is it true? Are you engaged?" Stephen's voice rose an octave. He turned a frank, disappointed face to Ellie.

"I-I...uh...why yes, I was...I am...I think."

"Yes, Ellie is engaged. She told me so herself...to a young man back in Chicago," Constance offered helpfully, unaware that to Robert and Ellie, "Chicago" meant something other than just a city.

"Yes, Chicago. That is true, isn't it, Ellie?" Robert reaffirmed in a low voice.

She turned to him for a moment. His eyes glittered as he stared at her.

"Em...yes...Chicago."

"And when will the marriage take place, Ellie?" Stephen's somber eyes met hers.

"Oh,...uh...soon...that is...um...when I return."

"I see," Stephen murmured. "I must extend my congratulations. How fortunate for you."

"Yes, very fortunate indeed." Robert chimed in with a narrowed gaze at Stephen.

"And what does your affianced do, Ellie?" Stephen ignored Robert. Ellie swallowed hard.

"He's a-an...investment banker."

"A banker?" Robert snapped. At his harsh tone, Ellie jerked her head in his direction. "How interesting." He eyed her with a curious glint.

"What exactly does an investment banker do, Ellie?" Malcolm had no idea how much further he dug Ellie's hole by pursuing the subject.

"He manages investments for clients. You know, stocks and bonds?" She couldn't remember. Did stocks and bonds exist at this time? Surely they did. The stock market crash would occur in thirty years.

"Ahh," Malcolm nodded. "Yes, of course. I was not familiar with that term."

Ellie discovered she could tilt her head slightly and

dip her hat in Robert's direction to block him from her line of sight, and she promptly did so. She looked over at Constance, who pressed her twitching lips together and raised a linen napkin to her mouth. By tipping her hat, Ellie exposed herself to Stephen more, but he didn't seem to be a problem.

Stephen gave her a regretful smile. There was nothing she could do, short of jumping up and announcing she was a fraud, but return his smile and resume eating.

"And how long has your betrothed been an investment banker, Ellie?"

Ellie acquiesced to good manners and turned her head slightly to allow him to see her face. Robert looked irritated with her ploy to avoid him, and she bit back a smile.

"About five years, I think." She tilted her hat once again.

"I see. I must say, Ellie, that is quite a fetching hat you are wearing. It certainly shades your face well...from the sun."

"Thank you," she murmured on a gurgle, with a raised eyebrow in Constance's direction. "I just bought it yesterday."

"Yes, you will remember I saw you and Constance shopping. Is this part of your trousseau?" he needled.

The man was impossible! Trousseau, indeed! Was she living in some gothic novel?

"Yes," she said shortly.

Stephen leaned in to speak in a low voice. "Well, it is lovely, Ellie. It matches your eyes perfectly. Your future husband is a very lucky man."

Ellie blushed. "Thank you, Stephen."

A small commotion occurred on her right, and she turned ever so slightly to see Robert pick up his chair and move it to his right, toward Constance. All eyes turned to him, and he smiled pleasantly at the group and sat back down. She watched a muscle in his jaw working and wondered how pleasant he really felt at the moment. He'd moved into Ellie's line of sight, and she could no longer avoid meeting his eyes, short of laying her head flat on the table.

"The sun...was in my eyes," Robert looked skyward.

No one commented on the fact that the day had grown cloudy, as Pacific Northwest days often did.

He turned bright green eyes on Ellie, who dropped her own gaze to her plate.

"And will we have the good fortune to meet your fiancé, Ellie? Will he visit Seattle in the near future?"

Ellie's head shot up. She couldn't remember where she was in her sequence of lies, so she took a chance.

"No," she replied evenly, fed up with the harassing line of questioning. "He will remain in Chicago. I'll be returning shortly."

"No, Ellie! When?" Constance's mournful note tugged at Ellie's heart. She was echoed by an equally saddened Stephen and Malcolm who joined in the chorus of "no." But it seemed Robert was finally silenced! His tightened lips and angry glare gave Ellie a small measure of satisfaction...or so she thought. She swallowed a lump in her throat the size of an apple.

She had to continue. "Soon, I'm afraid. I'm not sure exactly when, but it will be soon. My parents should send word any day now."

"I hoped you would stay longer," Constance murmured. Ellie watched Malcolm reach over to pat Constance's hand. "How can you face that long train trip again so soon, Ellie? Are you sure you cannot stay for a while?"

Ellie avoided Robert's eyes.

"Well, as you know, I lost all my things on the train, so I am just waiting for my parents to send money for my fare." Did that sound plausible, she wondered? "I must return to Chicago, where my fiancé is waiting for me."

Ellie's roving eyes passed over Robert's face. His jaw relaxed and his eyes softened. A gentle smile played on his lips.

"I am afraid this is the first I am hearing of this. Did you lose your luggage on the train?" Stephen turned to her with interest.

"I did not hear, either, Ellie. What happened?" Malcolm asked.

Ellie panicked for a moment. She couldn't remember what happened exactly. Involuntarily, she turned to Robert.

He came to the rescue. "Ellie's tickets, money and luggage were misplaced on the train, and I—my family and I, that is—had the good fortune to take her into our home until she could secure funds and other accommodations." He blithely ignored Ellie and Constance's startled looks.

"Ellie, how awful for you," Stephen said sympathetically. "Have they found your things yet?"

Ellie tore her eyes away from a complacent Robert and shook her head.

"No, I am afraid not."

"And how are you managing...that is...do you need...?" Stephen hesitated delicately. "May I offer some financial assistance in your time of trouble?"

"Well, of course...goes without saying." Malcolm cleared his throat. "Certainly, Ellie, if you need anything, I would be more than happy to help."

Ellie's face burned. She felt like a homeless beggar stomping her feet over a heated grate with a cup held out to passersby.

"No, I'm fine. I-I...uh...sold something, and I have enough money to cover my needs. I'm fine, thank you." She didn't miss the sharp look Robert gave her, but she kept her eyes on Malcolm and Stephen. Stephen nodded understanding and discreetly returned to his food. Constance looked mortified for Ellie.

"And what brought you to Seattle, Ellie? I am afraid I did not hear?" Malcolm seemed to have no idea that Ellie wished the earth would swallow her up.

She coughed on a sip of water and put her napkin to her lips before scanning the seemingly hundreds of eyes turned in her direction. Had she said?

"Umm...I...uh..." Ellie drew a blank. Was it possible for her to stand up and just start screaming? She would feel much, much better, though she wasn't certain where she would end up. Bedlam? Where was Bedlam, anyway? Probably England.

"Apparently, Ellie was on her way to Wenatchee to visit a favorite aunt. She fainted just as she descended the train. Unaware Wenatchee was her destination, we brought her back to our carriage, resulting in an unintentional kidnapping as we dragged her to

161

Seattle...thereby stranding her here." Robert shook his head with a glance at Constance. "Isn't that correct, Constance?"

Constance nodded slowly, her brow furrowed, confusion clouding her lovely eyes. "Yes, I do believe that is what transpired, though I did not know Wenatchee was her final destination. Is that so, Ellie?"

Ellie bit her lip and nodded, refusing to look at Robert. Although he'd rescued her once again, she thought his talent and ease with lying far surpassed her own abilities.

"Yes, that's about it." She pressed her napkin to her lips once again. "Well, Malcolm, I must say this has been a very pleasant meal. Thank you."

Ellie successfully moved the conversation away from herself, and Constance picked up the thread and moved into talk of the mundane.

The picnic ended within the hour, and Malcolm, Constance and Ellie said goodbye to Robert and Stephen as they made their way to Malcolm's carriage. Ellie remained silent on the ride home, exhausted from being under the interrogatory spotlight so long at lunch. She was fairly sure she'd managed to cross a few lies, though she couldn't remember which, and she hoped no one had noticed.

****

"Robert, surely you are not serious!"

Robert stared out the window of the parlor with his hands clasped behind his back.

"Oh, I most certainly am, Grandmother."

"But why this woman? There are so many others who are more... suitable?"

Robert glanced at his grandmother over his shoulder for a brief second with a wry smile. Then he turned away again to continue scanning the city below. It was as if he viewed it with new eyes.

"Suitable. Yes, what a word! I used that term myself once." His shoulders shook at the memory. "I sounded quite foolish."

"Well, I think it is an admirable word," Mrs. Chamberlain said, in a huff.

Robert turned away from his survey of the city with a

sigh. What was Ellie doing now, at this moment? He looked at his watch. He really needed to go in to the office. He'd been far too lax about his duties over the past few days. Robert sat on a green velvet chair and faced his grandmother.

"I am sure the word has its uses, Grandmother, but I cannot think of a single one right now."

She pursed her lips and narrowed her eyes.

"The woman ran away from you, from this house."

Robert smiled with a faraway look in his eyes. "Yes, she did, didn't she?"

"Robert, stop that daydreaming and pay attention."

"Yes, Grandmother?" He continued to smile, finding it extremely hard to draw his face into an attentive, grave expression.

"It seems quite likely she does not want to marry you, or she would not have left. And at any rate, there is no point to these romantic notions of yours. She is engaged to someone else." Mrs. Chamberlain sniffed and regarded her grandson with a raised brow.

"Yes, she does so say, does she not?" Robert flicked an imaginary speck of dust from his dark blue trousers. When he raised his head, he continued to smile.

Mrs. Chamberlain leaned forward. "Robert, did you hear me? Engaged! She is to marry another. Surely, you would not interfere in the betrothal promises of a woman, would you?"

Robert met her eyes but didn't really seem to see her. "Certainly not, Grandmother."

"Well then?" she pressed with exasperation.

"I think Ellie overstated the case. I feel certain she is not as betrothed as she describes."

"*Not as betrothed as she describes*? What foolish nonsense is that? Either one is engaged or one is not, young man!"

"Yes, I see what you mean. It does sound strange," he murmured with a bemused smile and another glance at his watch. Robert rose and bent over his grandmother to place a kiss on her cheek. "I must go in to the office today."

Mrs. Chamberlain clutched his hand and stared up at him.

"Robert, I don't wish to be unkind, but she is too...old...especially to begin a family."

Robert's smile broadened into a grin. He patted his grandmother reassuringly on the shoulder. "Old!" he repeated with a chuckle. "You have no idea, Grandmother. You have no idea." With shaking shoulders and a muffled laugh, he turned to leave the room.

Chapter Fifteen

Ellie had just finished a small lunch with Mrs.
McGuire when a knock on the door of the boarding house
announced the arrival of Melinda and Mrs. Chamberlain.
Melinda fell into Ellie's arms.

"Oh, Ellie, I am so glad to see you. Robert finally told
us where you were last night. I was certain he knew
where you were, but he said you needed time to yourself
and that we must not badger you."

"I'm so glad to see you, Melinda! And Mrs.
Chamberlain, how are you?"

"I would be better if I could sit down, my dear. Is
there a parlor? Could I have a cup of tea?" She surveyed
the foyer with an air of disinterest.

Mrs. McGuire, who'd been hovering in the
background, rushed forward. "Yes, of course, right this
way." She led the way into the parlor and settled Mrs.
Chamberlain and Melinda on the sofa. Ellie followed with
a sense of dread. For Melinda to visit her was one thing, a
pleasant surprise, but Mrs. Chamberlain's presence
seemed ominous.

"I will just run and get some tea," Mrs. McGuire
murmured as she plumped a throw pillow and set it on
the sofa next to the older woman.

Ellie threw her a grateful glance.

"I have never been to a rooming house before. It is
quite lovely." Melinda studied the sunny room with
interest. Her light blue velvet hat and matching wool suit
brought out the morning glory blue of her eyes. Mrs.
Chamberlain wore her usual conservative dark colors and
hat.

"It is, isn't it? I've never stayed in a boarding house
before, either. It's a lot of fun. There are three other young
women staying here. Dinner is always lively."

Melinda sighed. "It sounds wonderful...lively dinners
that is. Our house is quiet."

165

"There is nothing wrong with a dignified house, Melinda." Mrs. Chamberlain tapped her granddaughter's hand.

Melinda raised her eyes toward the ceiling for a moment, out of her grandmother's line of sight, and Ellie chewed on her lips.

"That is an unattractive habit, Ellie. Do not mutilate your lips so. They will thin and vanish soon enough. Perhaps sooner, in your case."

Ellie's eyes widened to match Melinda's. "I beg your pardon, Mrs. Chamberlain? Are you referring to my age?" She wasn't sure whether to laugh and cry.

Mrs. Chamberlain raised an eyebrow in Ellie's direction. "Of course I am. Youth and beauty are fleeting. You have very little of one and plenty of the other, but you must take care to preserve your complexion. Stay out of the sun, moisturize your face frequently, and do not make excessive facial expressions which will cause wrinkles. Smiling brings many lines to the mouth and eyes. You should attempt a more serene tilt of the lips rather than the toothy grin such as you favor us with now."

Against her will and better judgment, Ellie burst out laughing. "Oh, my goodness, Mrs. Chamberlain, I thought you were serious for a moment." Melinda watched the exchange between them with confusion. She smiled hesitantly at first, but sobered as soon as her grandmother spoke.

"I *am* serious, Miss Standish. My grandson is determined to ask you to marry him, and I cannot have my grandson's new wife looking older than half the ladies in town."

Ellie gasped and stared at the older woman. Melinda echoed the gasp, and her shocked eyes flew from her grandmother's stern face to Ellie's surprised one.

Just then the door opened and Mrs. McGuire sailed in with the tea. Ellie looked at her for a second and snapped her mouth shut. She thought she would kill for a drink at the moment, a nice stiff concoction of some mind-numbing liquor. Or maybe just an effervescent, mouth-tingling, brain-freezing, carbonated soda pop. Anything but tea, which always seemed to bring insanity in its wake.

Mrs. McGuire poured and passed out cups and saucers. Ellie received her tea with a shaking hand.

"Well, I will leave you to visit, then. I have dinner to see to." The door shut behind Mrs. McGuire, and the noise began.

"Look, Mrs. Chamberlain—"

"But, Grandmother, she is already engaged to—"

"I hardly know Rob—"

"They only met a few—"

"I have no intention—"

"Grandmama, how do you know—"

"Enough, girls!" Mrs. Chamberlain held up a hand.

Ellie stared open-mouthed, but Melinda seemed to know to clamp her lips shut.

"Now, just a min—" Ellie began hotly.

"Miss Standish. Please drink your tea and let me finish."

Ellie's eyes took in both women, and she obediently raised her tea to her lips and stared at Mrs. Chamberlain over the edge of the cup.

The older woman sighed. "I have talked to my grandson until I am blue in the face, and the boy seems set on his course. That you ran from his house in secrecy with a trifling excuse has done nothing to deter him. I have told him that you would not have hidden from him if you returned his love, but he will not listen. Melinda told me of your engagement, and I rallied with that information, but it seems he already knew of your betrothal and feels it lacks substance. The young man I once knew as a sensible, honorable gentleman seems to have vanished before my eyes, and I have you to blame, Miss Standish. The least you could do for me is stop that unbecoming biting of your lips as you again do now."

Ellie pressed her lips together and took another unladylike gulp of tea. Mrs. Chamberlain, two bright spots of red on her cheeks, did likewise. Melinda opened her mouth to speak and closed it. She reached for her tea and drank. The women eyed each other with mixed emotions.

Ellie lowered her cup and took a deep breath. "I'm sorry about Robert, Mrs. Chamberlain. I think he is infatuated with a stranger. I personally do not believe he

167

could have fallen in love in just a few days. I left the house because I knew I would be returning to Chicago fairly soon, and I could see that he was..."

"Falling in love?" Melinda offered helpfully.

Ellie shook her head, her cheeks burned. "For lack of a better term, yes. I thought it would help. I didn't mean to disappear like I did. Well, I did mean to, but I didn't mean to be disrespectful to you or hurtful to Melinda. I just didn't have the courage to face Robert." She bowed her head. "I am a coward."

"And the engagement?" Mrs. Chamberlain asked.

Ellie hesitated, no longer clear on her thoughts. "The engagement is cancelled."

Mrs. Chamberlain let out a hiss. Melinda put down her tea and clapped her hands with delight.

"Does Robert know?" she breathed.

Ellie shook her head. "I do not want him to know. I think it best he still believe I am engaged."

"But why?" Melinda's voice rose an octave.

"Because I still have to return to Chicago...to my life back there. I cannot stay here."

"Are you certain? Why can't you stay in Seattle?" Melinda asked with a dejected slump of her shoulders.

"Yes, I'm sure. I have responsibilities back there...my parents."

Melinda opened her mouth, but Mrs. Chamberlain interceded. "That is enough, Melinda. Do not press her any further. Ellie has explained herself sufficiently on that matter. It really is none of our concern."

Ellie shot the older woman a grateful look, but the older woman refused to meet her eyes and looked away toward the cold fireplace.

"Well, you must do as you think best, Ellie. I am sure my grandson will recover. As you say, it has only been a few days since you met."

"Exactly," Ellie murmured with a lump in her throat.

"Although, Mr. Chamberlain asked me to marry him the first night we met, and I said yes." Robert's grandmother met Ellie's startled eyes with her own bright blue gaze.

"Grandmama, I did not know that!" Melinda turned an appraising stare on her grandmother.

Ellie blinked. Was the older woman trying to tell her something?

"How wonderful for you!" she murmured.

Mrs. Chamberlain's cheeks turned pink. "Yes, it was quite romantic...really." Ellie watched her quick and unexpected smile droop. "I confess to being quite crotchety since he passed away ten years ago. I miss him a great deal."

"Oh, Grandmama." Melinda slid over next to her grandmother and kissed her cheek. "I am sorry."

"Yes, well, no need to crowd me on the sofa, child." She shooed Melinda, who moved over a few inches again, no small feat in her long skirts and corset.

"Well, then." Mrs. Chamberlain cleared her throat. "You will not reconsider having my grandson, is that correct, Ellie?"

Ellie couldn't bear the finality of the statement. Of course, she would consider him. She was head over heels in love with the man. And who wouldn't die to have such a handsome man pursue her so relentlessly? Or pursue the fantasy of a science fiction character, that is.

Ellie gave her head a slight shake.

"You have nothing to worry about from me, Mrs. Chamberlain."

"Oh, Ellie," Melinda mourned. Tears sprang to Ellie's eyes, and she gritted her teeth and stared straight ahead.

Mrs. Chamberlain rose. "I am not worried about you, Ellie, though if you do change your mind and marry Robert, you had better waste no time in having children."

"Grandmother!" Melinda giggled. "I cannot believe you—"

Ellie dashed the back of her hand to her eyes. "I'm not that old, Mrs. Chamberlain."

The older woman snorted and headed for the door. Melinda stopped to give Ellie a brief hug before following her grandmother out of the parlor. Mrs. McGuire bustled out from the kitchen to bid the guests farewell and then returned to her baking after ascertaining that Ellie planned to take a walk through the neighborhood.

Ellie climbed the stairs to her room and grabbed her jacket and hat. She jammed it on her head, wondering if the burning spots on her cheeks would ever fade back to their normal color. This adventure of hers kept her in a heightened emotional state of perpetual embarrassment, it seemed. She needed to get outside in the fresh air to think about things and make some plans.

Ellie stepped out of the house and looked up and down the street in every sense of the expression. The street was on an incline, as most things in hilly Seattle seemed to be. In need of a good workout, Ellie turned to the right to climb up the steep road.

As she walked and studied the "old" Victorian houses in their new condition, she wondered how best to extricate herself from the current problems. Though she had plenty of money for the moment, it would not last forever. Should she find a job teaching? Could she move to another town where Robert would never find her? Both possibilities seemed daunting in this particular day and age. One thing she'd noticed was a lack of the anonymity she knew in her own time. Everybody knew everyone's business here. She lifted her skirts over muddy patches on the walk and smiled. The modern expression seemed out of place.

The image of a train popped unbidden into her head, and she swore she could almost feel the rocking motion and hear the whistles blowing. Was that a message? Should she get back on a train for Chicago? Would that somehow return her to where she needed to be, where she was supposed to be? If Robert was right, and she had traveled through time, would that take her back in her own century? Did she want to return to her lonely existence?

Kyle was gone. That seemed clear. And if he wasn't gone, he would have to go, because she would never have fallen in love with Robert so readily, so completely, if she and Kyle had ever had a hope of a successful relationship.

What if by some miracle she stayed? Could she survive in the early 1900s, with virtually no women's rights, no financial means of her own, no airplanes, no television, no modern medicine? Did she even have the choice to stay?

Ellie looked up from the sidewalk to nod at a couple who strolled by. A carriage rolled down the street, while she could hear the horses' hooves of another carriage or wagon laboring up the hill behind her.

She shook her head. Ellie felt sure she could not stay. Be it a dream or some odd shift in a space-time continuum, she was going to wake up in her own bed soon, and all this would be gone. She sighed and paused to survey her surroundings with the colorful Victorian houses, lush gardens and tall evergreen trees. Turning around to capture the vista of the city which spread out below, she shrieked as she bumped directly into Robert's chest. She thrust her hands against him.

"Good gravy, what are you doing here? You scared me half to death."

Robert reached out to steady her, immaculate as always in a well-fitting gray suit and charcoal blue-gray vest.

"I am sorry. I did not mean to startle you. I meant to call out when I neared, but you turned so suddenly."

She eyed him narrowly and looked past him to see his carriage standing by, Jimmy staring discreetly off into the distance. "Why aren't you at work? Don't you ever go to work? I heard you were a workaholic."

He reared back and stiffened. "A workaholic? You mean drinking. I do not overindulge...well, except for the other night."

Ellie giggled. "No, *work*aholic...someone who works all the time. Dorothy told me you work all the time."

"Dorothy, eh? Yes, I have been known to work a great many hours. It has been my habit of many years."

"Why are you here, Robert? Your grandmother came to see me."

He sighed. "Yes, I know. I was afraid of that, and I wondered how you managed."

"I managed very well, thank you." Ellie fiddled with her skirt. "She had some interesting information for me."

Robert tightened his lips and turned away momentarily. "I hoped she would not mention our talk. She told you, then."

"Told me what, Robert?" Ellie closed her eyes for a moment. Would he actually say the words?

"That I intended to ask you to marry me," Robert murmured in a velvety voice.

Ellie opened her eyes and looked into his sparkling

171

green eyes, hating to extinguish the light. "I am engaged, Robert."

"No, you are not, Ellie."

Color flooded Ellie's face. "I most certainly am," she retorted. He couldn't possibly have seen his grandmother or Melinda in the last few minutes, could he? How could she have expected them to keep a secret?

"Then what is this?" Robert held her engagement ring in the palm of his hand.

Ellie gasped and fell back a step. "Where did you get that?"

"The pawn shop on Second Avenue, near the teashop where I saw you and Constance. It did not take much to deduce you had...ah...sold your *something* there." He looked down at the ring. "This is your engagement ring, is it not? What sort of betrothed woman sells her ring?"

"The sort who needs money," she snapped. "Did you pay the jeweler for that? I must owe you a fortune."

"You do not owe me anything. I will take it out in trade when we are married." His eyes danced merrily, and Ellie had all she could do not to fall into his arms.

"Your grandmother thinks I am too old," she muttered self-consciously.

"I love older women," he murmured, a seductive note creeping into his voice. He reached for her hand, but she snatched it away.

"I am leaving, Robert. I told you I cannot control this...this phenomenon. I'll be gone before you know it."

"Ah, yes, back to your parents in Chicago. You told me you were an orphan. Another fabrication, Ellie?"

She blinked and stared at him. "Oh dear, I did say that, didn't I? That's actually the truth. My parents are both dead." She quirked an eyebrow. "You certainly have quite the way with lies yourself, don't you? Wenatchee? On my way to visit a favorite aunt?"

Robert grinned. "I was only trying to help you out in an awkward situation...and very successfully, I might add."

Ellie chuckled. "Yes, very successfully. Thank you."

"Come, Ellie, come with me in the carriage. Let's drive around the city. I will take you to the waterfront this time, if you like." His dimples were irresistible.

Ellie hesitated. Under the hypnotic gaze of Robert's eyes, all her reasons for running from him seemed insubstantial and wispy. Why had she left, anyway?

With a smile, she put her hand in his, and he lifted her up into the carriage. Ellie put her fears aside for the afternoon as Robert set out to entertain and enthrall her with the sights and sounds of the city. He could have simply read a newspaper and she would have sat at his feet equally captivated by his charm. She kept her eyes on him as he described the city he loved, pointing out various lakes, parks, buildings and mountains. The afternoon passed all too quickly.

Robert left Ellie at her door just before dinner with a chaste kiss to her cheek, given that several pairs of feminine eyes peeked through the glass to observe them.

"I will come for you tomorrow, Ellie, in the morning." Robert turned and walked away. Ellie stared after him. *Come for her?* What did that mean, exactly? Were they going somewhere? Obviously Robert had not seen the latest murder films. "Come for you" meant something totally different to someone in a darkened theater clutching a bag of popcorn with an unsteady hand.

She entered the house and joined the women for another lively dinner, fielding questions as best she could about her morning visitors, as reported by Mrs. McGuire, and about her afternoon outing. She studied the girls with affection. Was this the rest of her life? No matter how many times she said she was leaving nor how many times she said she would wake up, she remained in the year 1901. Would she marry Robert? Was that even possible? Of course, he hadn't asked her. And children? Could she bear to have children, never knowing if she would wake up to lose them or leave them in time? Ellie shuddered. No, she could not bear that.

After dinner, she dragged herself up the stairs for bed, wishing for a moment that she had the solace of television to block her chaotic thoughts. As she undressed and climbed into bed, she wondered whether Robert was thinking of her as she now thought of him. She turned on her side to look out the window and gaze at the bright white moon, high in the sky. Her eyelids drooped and she slept.

****

Bright sunlight slipped through Ellie's half-closed eyelids. She turned over on her side to avoid the light. Her clock said 6:00 a.m. Clock? Ellie jerked and sat up. She was back in her bed in Chicago, the modern furnishings in the room all too sickeningly familiar.

"Honey, are you awake?" Kyle poked his head in from the bathroom, his blonde hair freshly washed and uncombed, a white towel draped loosely around his waist. Ellie had a sudden, wistful thought that she would never see Robert with a towel around his waist. Was it possible? Was her dream over?

Kyle moved toward the bed and bent to kiss her lips.

"Good morning, Ellie. I think you overslept this morning." He sat down on the edge of the bed and took her hand in his own.

Ellie stared at him in mute silence. Wasn't he gone? Hadn't he moved out? When had he returned?

"Kyle. I-I thought you left."

He looked at the clock and then back to her. "Nope, not me. I don't leave till 6:30. You know that." He patted her hand and stood up to return to the bathroom. He returned with a cup of coffee. "Made my own coffee this morning. Are you proud of me?"

Ellie nodded and pulled her knees up to her chest. "I mean I thought you...moved out."

Kyle turned a startled face to her. "What? What are you talking about?"

"I... Didn't you tell me that you were leaving...that you'd met someone? Was that a dream?"

Kyle eyed her like she'd lost her mind. And she had, there was no doubt of it. Where was Robert? He always seemed to understand her insanity. He wasn't the dream, was he? Surely *this* was the dream! Ellie felt a searing knife-like pain in her chest. She was afraid she knew the answer.

"Wow, that *was* some dream! Yeah, I left, but I came back, remember?"

"I thought..." Ellie grabbed a pillow and clutched it to her aching chest.

"Come to think of it, you *were* dreaming last night. A lot. You kicked a lot and talked and moaned and all sorts of things. I have to admit I finally moved to the couch to get some sleep." He jumped up and headed back to the bathroom.

Ellie bit back a sob. "What did I say?" she asked his retreating back.

"Oh, I don't know," he yelled from the bathroom. "Hard to make some of it out. Let's see. I heard Seattle, train, Victorian and a few names...Roger or Robert. You must have had quite the trip to Seattle last week."

"Last week?" she croaked.

He poked his head back out and stared at her. "Yeah, last week, remember? Seattle, the conference? The one you just got back from?"

Ellie rubbed her eyes with the palms of her hands. Real life had suddenly become a nightmare.

"Are you okay? Have a headache?" Kyle removed his towel and moved toward his closet to grab some clothes. Ellie looked up. She would never see Robert without clothes, would she? They would never live together. It was all a dream. She remembered waking up from dreams in the past and trying to recapture the moment. It never happened.

"No," she muttered. Ellie watched Kyle dressing, realizing with an aching finality that she could never marry him. He had never entranced her as Robert had with a look from his green eyes or a flash of his dimples. She suspected no living man ever could. Were she and Kyle even engaged any more? The idea seemed suddenly so foreign to her.

"Kyle?" she hesitated.

He turned from the closet. "Yes, Ellie?"

"I-I don't think I can marry you." She winced as she watched him. His reaction was unexpected in its lack of reaction. He turned away to pull on his trousers.

"I know, honey. You don't have to remind me. We talked about that already. You said after I came back that you weren't going to be able to marry me, and I told you that was okay. I'm obviously not the most faithful guy in the world, am I?" He gave her a sheepish grin and turned to the mirror to knot his tie.

"I'm sorry, Kyle." What she really longed to do was go back to sleep and find Robert.

He turned around and crossed over to the bed, bending to kiss the top of her head. "It's okay, Ellie. We've been through all this." He picked up her hand and studied it.

"Where's your ring? Did you put it away?"

Ellie stared at her hand. Had there been a ring? Really?

"I-I don't know. Didn't I give it back to you?"

Kyle shook his head and returned to the closet to grab his jacket. "Nope. I told you to keep it. I mean you've had it for what...two years now? It's definitely yours."

Ellie stared at her left hand. Where was the ring?

Kyle turned at the door and waved. "Better get up, Ellie. You're already late. I'll see you tonight."

As soon as the front door shut, Ellie jumped up and ran to her jewelry box. She rummaged through it, looking for her ring, but the shining diamond did not materialize from the clutter of costume jewelry. She retraced her steps and climbed back into bed, closing her eyes tight and burying her head under the covers. She tried deep breathing and counting sheep, but sleep eluded her. She pressed the pillow over her head and willed herself to sleep, to slip back into her dream, but the real world maintained its choking hold on her. She turned over. Hot tears poured from her eyes and ran down the sides of her face. *Please, please, please let me go back to sleep! Robert, you said you would come for me. Please come for me!*

An hour passed and still her inability to sleep kept the man of her dreams from her. Ellie pulled herself up in bed and sobbed into her hands. How could life hand her a magical romance and then take him away? She dragged herself out of bed and paced the apartment, pulling shades down to darken the rooms. She flopped into an easy chair and squeezed her eyes shut. She jumped up in seconds and went into the bathroom to search the cabinets for sleeping pills. There were none, of course. Sleep had never before been an issue.

Robert! Can you hear me? Robert!

Ellie returned to the bedroom and lay down on the floor, resting her burning face against the carpet, rubbing her face against the roughness. She thought she must be going insane. The world had gone quiet. Only the rumble of the El disturbed the dead silence.

The El! The train! Was it possible? Ellie jumped up and flew to the living room to flick on a lamp. She grabbed the phone book and phone and dialed the number for the train station, wading with bated breath through an endless, painful series of recorded telephonic menus while she sought for her answer. At one point, she banged the phone against the arm of her easy chair while she begged the recorded tinny voice on the other end to treat her like a human being. She had real questions, and she needed real answers. At last, the proper menu monotoned its arrival, and she waited forever to hear the information she wanted. With a quick glance at her watch, she jumped into some jeans, a sweater and tennis shoes, grabbed the cash from the cookie jar and flew down the stairs. Ellie had no idea where her purse and cell phone were, but she had no time to look for them. If she'd lost them in a dream, then where were they?

Ellie ran down the street for the El and raced onto the next train. She refused a seat as she paced from pole to pole waiting for the subway to reach the train station. She wanted to scream at the constant stops and starts, but she bit her lip and willed the El to move faster...if that were possible. They arrived at the train station, and Ellie jumped off the El and ran into the station. She hustled through the throngs of people and popped up to the ticket window, thanking her lucky stars she'd found one without a line. She paid for her ticket and ran down the concourse as she headed for the train that would leave in five minutes. Where was the gate? Where was the gate? Ellie's chest ached as she gasped for air. She felt lightheaded, as if she might pass out. Anxiety robbed her of oxygen. She stepped outside onto the platform and beheld her dear, beloved, gleaming silver train. There it was! The train that would take her once again to Seattle! Ellie knew it was a long shot, but it was all she had. She could not sleep. Perhaps Robert had not been a dream!

Chapter Sixteen

Ellie waved her ticket in the conductor's face and sped past him to hop aboard the train.

"31B, 31B," she muttered as if a woman possessed while she hurriedly scanned the seat numbers. "Where is it?"

"Aha!" she exclaimed to no one in particular when she located the seat she wanted. Luckily for someone else, it was empty, because Ellie had every intention of sitting in that seat. She slid into it and nestled against the window, hoping for a miracle.

Nothing happened. She squeezed her eyes shut and waited.

Still nothing. Ellie tried to regulate her erratic breathing. Her heart paused and skipped beats like Morse code. She willed herself to calm down.

"Not yet. Just wait," she murmured to herself. Passengers continued to board the train, and Ellie tapped her foot impatiently, hoping to see the last of them onboard and safely stowed in their seats so the train could leave.

Finally, the train began its stealthy movement, so unlike the jerking and whistle-blowing fanfare of the Victorian train in her dreams. She pressed her head against the cool glass and watched as the train tracks of Chicago fell away into the distance. Once they were out of the city, the train picked up its pace and Ellie closed her eyes, waiting for sleep.

Nothing happened. No sleep. No time travel. A single hot tear slid down Ellie's face and she brushed it away. She would not give up hope. There was still time. Reluctant though she was to leave her seat in case *it* happened, she had to use the bathroom. She hurried down the stairs and washed up, returning to her seat within minutes. As she settled in once again, Ellie wondered, had that been the moment? Had she missed the "window" by going to the bathroom?

The hours passed slowly as the train made its way through Wisconsin. By the time they reached Minnesota, she knew Kyle would be home from work and wondering where she was. She'd left no note for him. He might assume she'd stayed late at work. She often did. In fact, she realized she herself had been a workaholic—grading papers, preparing lectures, working on articles for publication. Just like Robert. The last week...or last night...had been one of the most restful of her life in terms of leisure time, though the stress of falling in love had been incredibly tense.

Ellie took a break from her vigil around eight that night and went down to the snack bar for a bite to eat. She returned to her seat with a sandwich and a surprisingly unexpected cup of tea and stared out the window at the passing lights. The tea wasn't nearly as tasty as that which she'd shared with Robert, but she had somehow grown fond of the ubiquitous beverage.

She closed her eyes as the train rolled out of St. Paul, Minnesota, and drowsed with her head lolling back and forth in the corner of her seat. She dreamed of a handsome silver-haired man with green eyes who visited his children in Washington, D.C. She awoke with a start and looked around. It was dark, but the rumbling sound of the tracks and a loud whistle revealed she was still on the train. What time was it? Where was her watch?

She reached out to the empty seat next to her. The sterile roughness indicated a polyester blend, not luxurious velvet. She squeezed her eyes shut against the burning tears, but they slid down her cheeks. She didn't bother to wipe them in the dark. Who would see?

She turned a miserable face to the window. Her grand idea to recreate the trip on the train was an abysmal failure. She was still here, on a modern train in her own time. Robert did not smile at her or take her hand under his arm. Melinda did not ogle her in curiosity. Mrs. Chamberlain did not disapprove. By Grand Forks, North Dakota, Ellie was numb. Nothing mattered. She might as well get off the train, but she lacked the energy to do even that. She'd already paid the fare to Seattle, and she found it easier to sit in misery than to get off the train

179

and call Kyle to send her money for a return trip home.

When the sun came up over North Dakota, Ellie stared at the Great Plains as the train rolled through wheat fields brightened to gold by the first rays of dawn. She blinked at the beauty of nature, and her spirits lifted...a little. The dark night had passed, and although Robert had not come for her, she felt better in the light of a new day.

"How are you doing, miss? Do you need anything?" The tall, young conductor leaned over to check her ticket. "Seattle, huh? Visiting family there?"

"Ummm...yes," Ellie murmured with a yawn. She stretched and wished her silver-haired gentlemen had joined her on this trip. She recalled dreaming about him the night before. What was his name? Edward? His eyes...so green...like Robert's.

The young conductor in wheel hat and dark blue jacket and vest consulted his wristwatch. "Well, the snack bar opens in a half hour, at 6 a.m. We reach Minot, North Dakota at 8:54 a.m. You can get off the train and stretch your legs there, if you like."

"Thank you," Ellie murmured. Did she want to stretch her legs in Minot, North Dakota? She had no earthly idea. On a modern train, she could stretch her legs by virtually running from car to car. Since the conductor had given her the idea, she stood at that moment and worked out the kinks in her knees. Another cup of tea and some breakfast might be in order.

Ellie spent the day wandering from car to car, studying the people on board. She wondered about their lives, who they visited, who they loved, whether they'd left anyone behind or were on their way to meet their true love. She hung around in the lounge car and stared out the panoramic floor-to-ceiling windows at the rolling fields of eastern Montana, a continuation of the Great Plains of North Dakota. She counted her money. Dangerously low on funds, she grabbed an inexpensive snack for lunch. She would be lucky to make it to Seattle before she ran out of money. Once there, she would call Kyle to book a hotel room for her and reserve her return fare...by airplane. She had no idea how she would explain her mad dash on the train, but she resolved to worry about that another time.

By evening, she dozed in her seat once again as they crossed into the Rocky Mountains.

"Mom, look, look! Up there! Look at those mountain goats!"

Ellie's eyes popped open at the young boy's shout from the seat behind. She peered out the window, and craned her neck to see three mountain goats hugging the side of a steep hill above the tracks. Well, to Ellie, they seemed to be "hugging" the mountainside. She suspected that, for mountain goats, they merely lazed about as a sunbather might do at a beach.

"Aw, Mom, why can't we stay here in Montana? I want to go to the Park."

The conductor strolled down the aisle intoning the next stop. "Essex, Montana. Essex, Montana. Glacier National Park." He didn't shout. He didn't have to. The modern train muted much of the rumbling along the tracks.

A woman's voice shushed the boy. "Quiet, Patrick. You'll wake the other passengers. Maybe we will go to the Park one day. Get some sleep now. We'll be in Seattle in the morning, and Grandma will be there to meet us."

The view of the mountain goats receded into the blue-gray dusk behind tall pine trees, and Ellie leaned her forehead against the cool window with her eyes closed. For a moment, she thought that it had actually happened. She'd traveled back in time! Young Patrick's voice sounded exactly like the little boy she'd heard just last week on the train...before she met her seat companion, Edward...and before she fell asleep to awaken to Robert.

But a quick glance around the darkening car revealed she was still on the same train—a comfortable but sterile silver snake that silently wound its way across the United States. She hugged herself and stared out of the window, willing the light to stay with her a little longer...to keep the long, dark night at bay. By breakfast, they would be nearing Seattle, and the trip would end. Her hopes of finding Robert would end.

Had Robert ever really lived? Or had he been a figment of her imagination? The aching sense of loss in her throat and chest seemed too real and painful to suffer over a mystical dream lover. She remembered the day she'd imagined Robert, Constance, Stephen and Malcolm dead and buried a hundred years later. The memory still made her shudder. Perhaps she could go to the library in Seattle and see if any of them had ever really existed. Perhaps find their graves? Was it possible?

Ellie brushed away the tears from her eyes with the back of her hands. She turned her face away from the aisle as a tall man approached. In the moment before she looked away, something about the waves of his dark hair caught her attention. She gasped and swung her head back in his direction.

The tall man glanced down at her, nodded pleasantly and passed.

It wasn't Robert! How could it be? She shook her head and pressed a hand to her racing heart. What was she thinking?

Ellie closed her eyes once again and dozed fitfully. During the night, she heard the conductor's monotone as he passed through the car with a quiet, "Spokane, Washington. Spokane, Washington." She pulled up her legs, hunched her shoulders and pressed tighter into her corner.

"Wenatchee, Washington, five minutes. Wenatchee, Washington."

Ellie pried open one eye to the faint rosy light of dawn. Her ears pricked. Wenatchee?

This was it! This had to be the moment. If she were ever going to find Robert, this had to be it! She jumped up from her seat, stumbling against the back of the seat in front of her. She had to get off at this stop. This is where Robert would be. She bent down to look out the window. Tall pine trees hugged the train tracks. Streaks of daylight broke through the openings in the forest. This had to be right.

The train slid into a smooth halt, and Ellie tripped down the stairs. She hopped off the train and surveyed the area around the concrete platform. Up and down the length of the gleaming train, other passengers descended to stretch their legs. Something was wrong. Nothing looked as it should.

She turned to the young conductor who stood by the

door of the car. "Excuse me. Is this Wenatchee?" The modern concrete platform, paved parking lot and steel and glass station bore little resemblance to the old wooden station surrounded by dirt.

"Yes, ma'am." He pointed to the sign over the station which read "Wenatchee" in glaringly huge letters. Ellie stared at it for a moment, and her exhausted knees wobbled. Then Wenatchee wasn't the answer! Robert did not appear. He didn't stride up to her and take her hand in his. He didn't fold her in his arms.

Ellie's feet began to move with a will of their own, and she headed toward the train station. A large round station clock read 5:35 a.m. She pushed open the glass and steel door and stepped into the deserted lobby. Modern acrylic benches in a multitude of colors decorated the room. No one waited for her. The lobby was desolate. This was her last hope! Gone!

A bout of dizziness and a wave of nausea overtook her. Her knees buckled and she fell against one of the benches. She gave in to a strange urge and laid her head down for just a moment, hoping the world would soon right itself. But the world continued to slide, and Ellie slipped into unconsciousness.

"Miss. Miss, are you all right? Did you fall asleep?"

Ellie woke up to gentle prodding of her shoulder by a kindly, bespectacled, gray-haired man sporting a train conductor's uniform. She tried to raise her aching head but slumped for a moment.

"I-I'm fine. I'm okay. What time is it?" she asked assuming only a few moments had passed.

"It's 5:45 a.m., Miss. The station is closed. How did you get in here?"

Ellie met the older man's kind blue eyes and looked behind him to see weathered wooden walls and a dusty floor. The varnished pine bench under her legs bore no resemblance to the acrylic bench onto which she'd slumped. Her heart began to pound.

This was it! She'd done it!

The loud whistle of the train brought her to her feet. She rushed past the startled stationmaster and pushed open the wooden door, careening to a halt. The train no longer stood in front of the station. A puff of black smoke was all that remained of the gleaming black vintage train as it barreled out of the station on its way to Seattle.

"Wait!" Ellie screamed as she ran across the dusty wooden platform toward the empty tracks. She stopped for a moment and bent over, bracing her hands on her knees to draw in a deep breath.

"Wait!" she screamed even louder. "Wait for me!" Her throat burned, but she kept screaming. "Robert! Wait for me! Please don't leave me! Robert! Come back for me!"

"Ellie, wake up!" Strong arms enveloped her.

Chapter Seventeen

"Ellie, wake up!"

She awoke with a start, tears streaming down her cheeks, and burrowed her face into Robert's neck. He held her against him and kissed the top of her head as he rubbed her back in long soothing strokes.

"Another dream, my love?"

Ellie nodded, rubbing against his warm skin.

"Were you running for the train again, sweeting?"

Ellie calmed to the rumble of his voice in his chest.

"Again," she murmured. She drew a deep breath to calm her racing heart. "I still haven't caught it," she said with a watery chuckle.

Robert's low laugh bounced her face on his chest, and she craned her neck to look at him. He bent his head and kissed her lips in a slow, lingering caress, pulling her closer to him, molding her body against his as they lay together. He lifted his head and studied her face with warm green eyes.

"Maybe the dreams will end someday, my love. I hope so."

She buried her face against him again. "I hope so too," she mumbled. "I don't think they're good for the baby."

Robert slid his hand down to her rounded stomach. "The baby will be fine, Ellie. She has been a hundred years in the making. She must be strong, don't you think?"

Ellie chuckled at Robert's logic. "Yes, dear. I think he will be very strong." She leaned up on one elbow and stared into her husband's soft, dark-lashed eyes. "I love you, Robert. I cannot tell you how much I love you."

"And you are the only woman I have ever loved, Ellie. I waited for you a long time." He stared at her as he reached to brush the tangled curly brown hair from her face. "I hope the baby looks like you. I hope she has your

185

hair."

Ellie grinned. "Well, your grandmother just hopes I have a baby with two arms and two legs. You know she thinks I'm too old."

Robert smiled and his eyes twinkled. "If only she knew *how* old. Almost one hundred and fifty years, I would say." He snorted. "You look remarkable for your age, Mrs. Chamberlain."

She gave him a playful smack on his shoulder. "Thank you, Mr. Chamberlain."

His face grew serious. "Thank you, Ellie, for marrying me and having our child. Thank you for coming back in time for me."

Ellie wrinkled her nose. "You know I still don't believe in time travel, Robert, though it appears likely that this isn't a dream. No one could possibly dream up a man like you...the love we've shared...the nights." Her face burned at the light in his eyes. She looked down on her rounded belly. "And the baby we created together."

"This is no dream, my love. Though Mr. Wells wrote back to tell me he thought I had taken his book a little too seriously, *I* know you heard my loneliness and came through time for me."

She pressed her lips against the adorable cleft in his chin and tilted her head to study his face.

"I can't imagine how a handsome man like you could ever be lonely, Robert."

His eyes narrowed seductively. "Well, it took you forever to come to me. I waited and waited, though I understand you had quite a long journey."

Ellie laughed, and the baby in her stomach moved in response. She lay back and reached for Robert's hand to place it on her stomach. He rolled over on his elbow and looked down into her face. His green eyes sparkled, reminding her of another set of eyes.

"Robert. Do you think it's possible that I could have met my grandchildren in the future? There was a man on the train..." She let her voice trail off as Robert began to kiss the corner of her mouth.

****

Edward awoke to the voice of the conductor. "Wenatchee, Washington. Wenatchee, Washington."

He rubbed his eyes and turned to look at his seat mate. She was gone. He checked his watch. 5:45 a.m. The hour was early. Muted light broke through a few cracks in the curtains. Maybe she'd gone to the restroom.

He stood to stretch his legs with a fervent wish that he could get a cup of tea at this early hour, but the snack bar would not open for another fifteen minutes. He eased himself back into his seat and waited for the young woman...Ellie...to reappear. Maybe she would like to join him. There was something about her that captured his interest. He wasn't certain what it was. The color of her hair, the hazel of her eyes, the tilt of her lips as she smiled?

Edward studied her empty seat for a moment and suddenly he jerked.

Ellie! Good gravy! That was his grandmother's first name! How had he not remembered that? The name was not that common. He'd always just thought of her as "Grandma." He shook his head with a bemused smile. What a coincidence.

Edward turned to the window and watched the first rays of dawn streaking through the tall pine trees of his home state. Memories flooded in as he recalled his youth, playing at his grandparents' house on the hill...the house he still owned. He smiled as he remembered his grandmother's odd mode of dress for gardening—an old skirt she fondly referred to as her "jeans skirt" and the open-backed shoes she'd called "clogs," as if she were some Dutch woman. How odd that both styles had recently come back into fashion. The cyclical nature of fashion!

He and his older sister had adored spending time with their eccentric grandmother and doting grandfather. No one else had grandparents quite like them, but all their playmates envied them the big house with nooks and crannies suitable for playing hide-and-seek and a sloping lawn that turned into a wonderful sled hill on rare snow days. Grandma Ellie had always been the first to acquire any new gadgets on the market—the first car, the first radio, the newest kitchen appliances. She and Grandpa had taken them on their first train trip to Glacier National Park, where she'd shown them mountain goats and old historical trains like the one where she had

187

met Grandpa.

Great Aunt Constance had often said that he looked just like a younger version of his grandfather. Uncle Malcolm agreed. He always agreed when Aunt Constance spoke. She and Great Aunt Melinda often speculated whether he would grow to be as tall as the handsome silver-haired man he'd worshiped. And he had. Edward stretched out his legs.

Grandma Ellie used to make him blush whenever she bent down and peered into his eyes. He was never quite sure what she was looking for, but she always smiled, kissed his forehead and told him he was the "spitting image of Grandpa and would some day grow to become a handsome old gentleman."

Edward smiled at the memories. Grandma Ellie had always been ahead of her time, full of new ideas, controversial thoughts and strange colloquialisms...for the time. He remembered whispers from other parents behind covered hands, but his grandparents shook their heads and kept laughing.

He looked at his watch again. 6:00 a.m. The snack bar was open, and still the young woman had not returned. Neither did he see any of her possessions. He stood and scanned the boarding passes above the seats. Only his pass remained. She said she was going to Seattle. Where had she gone? Had she ever even been on the train?

He shook his head and smiled. He moved down the car toward the snack bar. Maybe she had just been a dream.

About the Author...

Bess McBride began her first fiction writing attempt when she was 14. She shut herself up in her bedroom one summer while obsessively working on a time travel/pirate novel set in the beloved Caribbean of her youth. Unfortunately, she wasn't able to hammer it out on a manual typewriter (oh yeah, she's that old) before it was time to go back to school. The draft of that novel has long since disappeared, but the story is still simmering within her, and she will get it written one day soon.

Bess was born in Aruba to American parents and lived in Venezuela until her family returned to the United States when she was 12. She couldn't fight the global travel bug within her and joined the U.S. Air Force at 18 to "see the world." After 21 wonderful and fulfilling years traveling the world and gaining one beautiful daughter, she pursued her dream of finally getting a college education. Armed and overeducated, the gypsy in her has taken over once again, and she is now embarking on a full-time journey in a recreational vehicle as she continues to look for new adventures and place settings for her writing. The Wild Rose Press has helped her fulfill a lifelong dream of writing romances.

Visit Bess' website at www.bessmcbride.com

Excerpt from *Love of My Heart* by Bess McBride:

"So how are you today, Bill?" Aggie asked the strikingly handsome but totally ineligible dark-haired, dark-eyed man sitting in the wingback chair across from her. As always, she tried to filter out her attraction to him and focus on the words spoken between them.

"Good, Aggie. How are you doing?" he asked with interest. He gazed at her intently with mesmerizing dark brown eyes....

Excerpt from *A Sigh of Love* by Bess McBride:

Abbie opened her eyes and found a tall man standing in the aisle next to her seat. Startled, she blinked and met a pair of almond-shaped, obsidian eyes that crinkled at the corners. His friendly smile widened to a grin.

"May I?" he asked, indicating the window seat past her.

"Oh, sure." Abbie quickly scrambled out of her seat and stepped into the aisle to allow him to pass. She caught her breath when he slid past her to take his seat. His face was strikingly handsome. Exotic eyes were the prominent feature in an angular bronze face with a narrow nose and full lips.

As the plane rolled onto the runway, Abbie leaned her head back and closed her eyes for a moment. It wasn't too late. She could still jump up and ask the attendants to stop the plane and let her off. She smiled, imagining the scene. Would they open the doors and let her out onto the runway to trudge back to the terminal on foot? Would they take the airplane back to the terminal and boot her out the door—forbidden ever to book a flight with them again? A quiet hysterical giggle escaped her wayward lips. Or would they force her to inexorably march on and continue the flight to Anchorage against her will?

Printed in the United States
128839LV00001B/34-54/P